Trouble in the County

Texas Ranger Mike Hart rode grimly on the trail of the notorious outlaw Gimp Alder, with orders to take him dead or alive. Alder was heading back to Mexico and Hart was determined to stop him.

The trail was long and arduous for Hart – until he reached Blackthorn County. There he caught up with Alder and took him alive, thinking his troubles were over. Little did Hart suspect they were only just beginning. There was trouble brewing in the county and it fell to him to deal out the law with his usual vigour.

With murder stalking the county and greedy men determined to have their way, Hart would have to go all out to stop them.

By the same author

Range Grab
Bank Raid
Range Wolves
Gun Talk
Violent Trail
Lone Hand
Gunsmoke Justice
Big Trouble
Gun Peril
War at the Diamond O
Twisted Trail
Showdown at Singing Springs
Blood and Grass
Twisted Trail
The Hanna Gang

Trouble in the County

CORBA SUNMAN

A Black Horse Western

ROBERT HALE · LONDON

© Corba Sunman 2005
First published in Great Britain 2005

ISBN 0 7090 7718 1

Robert Hale Limited
Clerkenwell House
Clerkenwell Green
London EC1R 0HT

Typeset by
Derek Doyle & Associates, Shaw Heath.
Printed and bound in Great Britain by
Antony Rowe Limited, Wiltshire

ONE

Texas Ranger Mike Hart reined in quickly when he reached the rim of the gully and saw a stream meandering through it. He dropped his right hand to the butt of his holstered Colt .45 as he looked around, his keen blue eyes searching instinctively for likely ambush spots, his mind filled with the tensions of the manhunt he was on. It was only when he felt certain he was alone that he let his attention switch to the saddled horse standing forlornly by the water's edge on the far bank and the prone figure of the man lying with his face half-submerged in the fast-flowing stream.

A sigh escaped Hart as he hesitated. He had enough problems without sticking his nose into anything that did not concern his current assignment. The man looked dead – had evidently been slaking his thirst when a bullet hit him between the shoulder-blades. Hart could see the bright splotch of blood which had spread through the light-blue shirt the man was wearing, and judged that the ambusher had been in cover on the opposite side of the stream.

The killer had allowed his victim to get down for a drink before shooting. It looked like cold-blooded murder, and Hart wondered if Gimp Alder had deliberately killed a stranger to slow the pursuit of the Ranger he knew to be on his tail.

Hart stepped down from his saddle – a big man, wide-shouldered and tall, his weathered face angular with prominent cheekbones. He was dressed in faded blue denims, a black shirt under a leather vest, and his long legs were encased in narrow shotgun chaps. A dusty black Stetson was pulled low over his keen blue eyes.

He trailed his reins and lifted his Winchester from its fringed scabbard under the right side of his saddle. The black sniffed in the direction of the water, but turned away to graze. Hart moved fast for a big man. His feet found a well-defined game trail and he descended the side of the gully, leading the black by its reins.

He had been trailing Gimp Alder for two weeks now, and the killer was as slippery as his reputation professed him to be. Twice he had been close enough to toss rifle slugs at the killer, but Alder knew all the tricks of his murderous trade, and had stayed just far enough ahead to elude capture, although there were signs that he was close to the point of turning at bay in an attempt to rid himself of the deadly nuisance dogging his trail.

Captain Ed Buckbee, commanding D Company, Texas Rangers, had warned Hart that Alder would be no push-over. The killer had eluded two Rangers the year before, killing one of them before disappearing into the badlands along the Texas/New Mexico border. Months later, Alder came back east to rob a Wells Fargo Overland coach in Texas, killing the driver and the shotgun guard in the process. Hart had drawn the duty of locating the killer and taking him, dead or alive.

Hart reached the motionless figure by the water's edge but did not stop. He crossed the stream and entered the brush on the further side to search for signs of the ambusher, finding the spot where a man had lain in wait for some considerable time. He picked up a brass cartridge-case which had been ejected from a Winchester 44.40 and slipped it into a breast-pocket before moving away from the stream.

He searched around, saw Alder's prints heading away from the gully, and then found the spot where the ambusher had left his horse in thick brush. He noted deep hoofprints in smooth dust and squatted to study them. They had not been left by the horse Gimp Alder was riding. When he arose he was certain he would recognize the stranger's prints should he see them again.

Satisfied that the ambusher had departed, Hart went back to the body at the water's edge and dropped to one knee to examine it. The man was wearing good range clothes, and looked to be middle-aged. His long brown hair was streaked with grey. Hart estimated that he had been dead for at least two hours. He stood up to check the man's horse, and became aware that he was being watched by a rider sitting a roan up on the rim roughly at the spot where Hart himself had come upon the scene.

The man was holding a rifle and the weapon was covering Hart.

'Come down and take a look at this man,' Hart called, holding his rifle with the muzzle pointing at the sun-baked ground.

After a slight hesitation, the stranger spurred his horse forward and descended the bank into the gully. The muzzle of his rifle did not waver from Hart's big figure. He reined in but did not dismount. He was not old, in his late twenties, and suspicious. His brown eyes were narrowed and he was taking no chances. He did not look at the dead man.

'Who are you?' he demanded. 'That's Luke Warner lying there, dead, by the look of him. Did you kill him, stranger?'

'He's been dead about two hours.' Hart lifted the left lapel of his leather vest to reveal his Ranger badge, a small silver star set in a silver circle. 'I'm Mike Hart, D Company, Texas Rangers. I'm trailing the outlaw Gimp Alder. He passed through here about two hours ahead of me, and he knows I'm on his trail. But all the signs are that Alder didn't kill this man. This is Luke Warner, huh? Tell me about him.'

'He's foreman of K Bar, owned by Grat Kane. I'm Al Denton. I own the Rafter D west of here. I'm on my way to town, which is ten miles to the south-east.'

'What town is that?' Hart asked.

'Mesquite. You're in Blackthorn County, in case you aren't aware of it.'

'I know roughly where I'm at.' Hart glanced around and could see low, brushy hills far off to the west. He figured Alder was making for Blanco Pass on his murderous way back to Mexico. 'Are you riding into Mesquite? If you are, I'll give you a hand to put Warner across his saddle and you can take him in. Who's running the law there?'

'Deputy Sheriff Lew Seifert. Sheriff Moore is over in Canyon City, the county seat, fifty miles west of here.'

'Tell Seifert you met me. Ask him to wire Ranger headquarters in Austin and report my position. I'm within striking distance of Gimp Alder and expect to get him in the next day or so. Tell Seifert I'll swing over to Mesquite when I'm done with Alder.'

'Sure. Good luck, Hart. I've heard of Alder. He's one tough *hombre*.'

'They don't come any tougher, but I've got him on the run. He ain't so tough that he'll stand and fight.'

Denton thrust his rifle into its scabbard and they lifted the dead man across his saddle in a face-down position. Denton roped him in place.

'I hope you get your man.' Denton swung into his saddle and wrapped the reins of the dead man's horse around his saddle horn. He lifted a forefinger to the brim of his Stetson and rode off, splashing across the shallow stream.

Hart watched Denton until the rancher and his grim burden had disappeared out of the gully, then took hold of his reins and led the black to the water's edge. While the animal was drinking, he moved upstream several yards and dropped flat to slake his own thirst. When he'd finished he arose to stop the animal drinking more than was good for it. He rode up the opposite slope of the gully and went on, taking up Alder's tracks and following them patiently.

He rode steadily, aware that he could follow Alder for longer than the man could run. For three hours he rode through the brush, following the faint trail that marked the progress of his quarry. His gaze constantly searched his surroundings, watching for the first sign of an ambush – the glint of sunlight on a rifle barrel, birds rising, or a jackrabbit running alarmed from any thick clump of brush.

When he spotted a ranch headquarters ahead he sat his horse on a hilltop about a quarter of a mile distant and took a pair of field glasses from a saddle-bag to study the quiet scene. He saw a number of adobe buildings, all single-storey and looking drab and unlovely in the bright sunlight. Several figures were moving around the big yard, intent on their ranch chores. There was a guard sitting a horse just inside the gate which gave entrance to the big yard in front of the largest building of the headquarters.

Hart checked the ground before him and his lips pulled into a thin line when he saw that Gimp Alder's tracks led straight into the ranch. He was aware that the outlaw had friends here and there all the way to the Mexican border, and wondered if Alder had gone to ground at last. He nudged his horse into motion again; knowing that there was only one way to find out if Alder had turned at bay.

As he rode in he noted details of the ranch, which was a big outfit, judging by the number of barns and pole corrals. Then he saw a board over the gateway, and his eyes narrowed at the sight of K Bar burned into the wood with a hot running-iron. This was the ranch where the dead man, Luke Warner, had been foreman.

Hart was seen long before he reached the gate and by the time he got there six men were standing in a group awaiting his arrival. Without exception, they carried rifles in addition to their holstered pistols. They were silent, alert, primed for trouble. The guard gigged his mount forward a couple of paces, his rifle balanced on his saddle horn, its muzzle covering Hart.

'What's your business?' the man asked.

'I'll tell that to your boss,' Hart replied.

'He ain't home to any saddle tramp riding the grub line,' the guard rapped. 'You better keep moving, mister. Now ain't a good time to horn in here.'

'Grat Kane owns this spread, huh?' Hart persisted.

'Who wants to know, and why?'

'I'm Mike Hart, Texas Ranger. Kane will see me.'

'You got proof who you are?' The guard did not relax. His cold gaze was filled with suspicion.

Hart revealed his Ranger badge and the tension gripping the group of waddies evaporated slightly. Rifles were lowered and feet shuffled. Two of the men turned away instantly.

'Hold it right there,' Hart rapped, and all movement ceased. 'Who's ridden in here during the last two hours?'

'Ain't seen a soul,' the guard said. 'Folks in this county know we don't hang out no welcome signs.'

Hart reached down, opened the gate and thrust it

wide. He rode into the yard, scattering the assembled men as he nudged his horse towards the big house. He noted Alder's tracks veering away towards a distant corral and studied the barns and shacks for signs of movement, reluctant to give Alder an edge. He saw no cause for alarm and continued until he reined up in front of the ranch house.

A giant of a man emerged from the deep shadows inside the house and halted on the porch, feet apart and arms akimbo. He was several inches over six feet, and looked to be about six feet around the waist. His dull grey shirt was straining to cover his massive body. He was wearing size twelve riding boots, and an outsize black Stetson was perched atop his wiry black hair. His moon-face was more than half-covered by an unkempt black beard that gave him a wild look. His gun belt seemed to have been made up from two ordinary belts stitched together, and the holster on his right thigh contained a .45 Colt. His right hand did not stray far from the butt of the pistol.

'What in hell are you doing in my yard?' The man's voice was unnaturally low-pitched, sounding as if it came up from his boots. 'Did that no-account Callum let you through that gate after I gave orders no one was to get in?'

'He tried to stop me,' Hart replied, 'but I guess he reckoned it would be too dangerous.'

'So you bluffed your way past that bonehead. Well, that's easy enough to do. What's your business? If you're looking for a riding job then you're wasting your time, and mine.'

'You're Grat Kane?'

'None other. What do you want?'

'I was told that Luke Warner is your foreman.'

'Yeah. Why didn't you say you've got business with Luke? Any friend of Luke is a friend of mine. But he ain't here right now. He's gone into town – won't be back for a couple of days.'

'I'm Mike Hart, Texas Ranger. Warner won't be coming back. I found him lying in a stream a few miles from here. He'd been shot in the back; was dead a couple of hours when I found him.'

'Dead? Bushwhacked?' Kane's jaw dropped in shock and his eyes opened wide. 'How'd you know it is Luke?'

'Al Denton came up when I was checking Luke and filled me in on the details. Denton was heading for Mesquite, and took the body in to report to the local law.'

'Poor Luke bushwhacked!' Kane groaned. 'I reckon I know who did it, too.'

'Who?'

Kane smiled and the left side of his mouth pulled downwards, as if a muscle was not working normally. His lips peeled back, revealing black, broken teeth. He shook his massive head as an ominous chuckle emerged from his throat.

'Never mind. I'll take care of Luke's killer. What are you doing around these parts?'

'Trailing an outlaw, and I'm about two hours behind him. His tracks led me into your yard.' Hart waited then, his keen gaze on Kane's rugged face.

'An outlaw rode into this yard?' Kane shook his head. 'This ain't the time to be funning, Ranger, with

13

poor Luke being toted into town like a piece of butchered meat. You should have some respect for the dead.'

'I've been following Gimp Alder's tracks for more than two weeks, and I know them better than the back of my hand. Alder came into your yard and headed for the corral on the far left. I questioned your men at the gate and they denied anyone had ridden in. That means they're lying. They're hiding the fact that Alder was here – might still be, and I wanta know why.'

'The hell you say! If that's the truth of it then I'll wanta know why myself.' Kane came to the edge of the porch and yelled stridently. 'Callum, get over here, and make it quick.'

The rider on guard at the gate wheeled his horse and approached at a canter. He reined up in front of the porch beside Hart.

'What's on your mind, boss?' he asked. 'I ain't got a thing to report. The place is as dead as Boot Hill.'

'The Ranger says an outlaw rode in here this morning.'

'I ain't seen hide nor hair of anyone looking like an outlaw, boss.'

'Don't get smart with me, Callum, or you'll be picking your teeth out of the dust. The Ranger just told me Luke was bushwhacked a couple of hours ago. He's on his way to town right now, face down across his saddle. Where's that rider who came into the yard earlier?'

'He stopped by the cook-shack for a bite to eat and some coffee, and then lit out again, heading west,' Callum said.

'Why did you lie to the Ranger?' Kane growled in his beard. 'Don't you know better than that?'

'The guy said he was being followed by someone who tried to rob him yesterday. He asked me to tell anyone who came in that he hadn't been here.'

'Get the hell back to your job, and do it right or you can ride out permanent.'

Callum grinned and wheeled his mount. Hart watched him riding back towards the gate before returning his attention to the big rancher. Kane was watching him intently, his dark eyes glinting under the wide brim of his Stetson.

'You got some kind of trouble around here?' Hart asked.

'No. What makes you think that?'

'You got a guard watching the place, and when I rode in a number of your crew came to the gate, carrying rifles. They were loaded for bear. Apart from that, Luke Warner was murdered this morning.'

'There ain't been no trouble around here.'

'So why did you say you knew who killed Warner?'

'Luke had some enemies. I'll be looking them up.'

'Mind if I check out those tracks crossing your spread?'

Kane shrugged his heavy shoulders. 'You're the law, ain't you?' He showed his teeth in a grin that was more like a snarl.

'I wonder, sometimes.'

'Well, I'm a law-abiding man. Sure you can look around. I got nothing to hide. Let me know if there's anything else I can do for you.'

'Thanks. So long.'

Hart turned his horse away from the house and picked up Alder's tracks leading off to the cook-shack. He paused at the door of the shack and a short, fat man appeared from inside, wiping his hands on a dirty cloth.

'Like a cup of coffee?' he demanded.

'Thanks.' Hart stepped down from his saddle and stood in the doorway, turning slowly to look around the yard. He saw ranch hands watching him from the nearest barn and one of the corrals.

The cook reappeared, holding a cup of coffee.

'Thanks.' Hart took the drink. 'I'm the second stranger in here today, huh?'

'There was another, sure.' The cook nodded. 'He was in an all-fired hurry. Said someone was on his back trail who could give him a lot of trouble if he caught up. That would be you, huh?'

'Yeah. I'm Mike Hart, Texas Ranger. I'm trailing Gimp Alder the outlaw. Can you describe the man who was here before?'

'Tall guy. Big. Looked like trouble in the flesh. He walked with a limp, favouring his right leg.'

'That's Alder. How long ago did he pull out?'

'Like I said, he was in a real hurry. Swallowed a plate of beef and beans and some coffee before he lit out beyond that corral, heading south-west, mebbe two hours ago.'

Hart drank the coffee and returned the cup to the cook.

'Thanks. So long.'

He mounted and set off towards the corral, following Alder's tracks. The outlaw had left the ranch at a run, his horse leaving deep hoofprints in the dust. Hart heaved a sigh when he reached open range beyond the ranch and pushed his horse into a canter before increasing to a run, keenly aware that it was about time he brought Alder's crooked career to an end.

Alder's tracks went on and on, leading into the south-west, and Hart followed patiently. Three hours passed and the ground began to change almost imperceptibly. The undulating range was giving way to the low brushy hills he had seen on the horizon early that morning. Alder's tracks were still in evidence, and Hart divided his attention between them and his surroundings, aware of the great danger that Alder might suddenly decide he had run far enough and halt to set up an ambush.

His sharp gaze suddenly picked out a horse huddled on the ground some fifty yards ahead, and he reined aside immediately, suspecting a trap. He rode into cover and lifted the field glasses to his eyes. The horse was dead, its left foreleg broken, and the animal had been shot in the head. It was Alder's horse. Hart felt a twinge of satisfaction at the knowledge that his man was afoot.

He rode forward slowly, right hand at his hip, close to the butt of his pistol. His eyes were narrowed, and he was ready to slip into action at the first sign of trouble. Alder couldn't go anywhere without a horse and the outlaw knew exactly where he could get a good replacement – Hart's own mount.

Reaching the horse, Hart saw Alder's footprints

heading away from it, leading towards the nearest high ground. He followed eagerly. The outlaw had left his saddle. He was afoot and had nowhere to run or hide. Hart proceeded cautiously, aware that Alder would not surrender peaceably.

Hart reached the top of the hill without sighting his quarry and reined in to take stock of his surroundings. His lips pulled into a thin line when he spotted a shack in the brush a hundred yards ahead. A pole corral was situated to the left of the little building. Chickens were scratching in the dust, and a milk-cow stood in the shade of an open-sided byre, tail swishing and its head low.

Hart studied the scene. There were no other signs of life. The silence was heavy, brooding. Heat lay like a physical barrier upon the dusty range. He remained motionless for interminable minutes, checking out the area, bringing his field glasses into play again, and tensed when he picked out the crumpled figure of a man lying in the open doorway of the shack in the careless attitude of one who was dead.

Alder had left his calling-card. Hart nudged the horse forward and edged sideways to descend the hill on the left. He reached level ground and kept moving to the left, assuming that Alder was still in the shack. When he was within twenty-five yards of the shack he dismounted and drew his pistol to check its loads. He wrapped his reins around a branch of a bush and took his rifle from its scabbard.

He was about to go forward to check out the shack when a woman screamed inside it, the thin sound of terror echoing through the heavy silence. Hart cocked his pistol. He saw movement in the doorway, and then a small figure appeared, leaping over the motionless man lying there and running furiously away from the building.

A rifle barrel appeared in the doorway and fired a single shot even as Hart threw up his gun hand. The running figure fell heavily as the report of the shot hammered and echoed. Hart held his fire. The rifle was withdrawn. Dust drifted from the spot where the figure had fallen.

Hart eased away to the left, moving slowly towards the shack. A glassless window was facing him and he covered it with his pistol. Echoes were grumbling away across the limitless range. The woman screamed again. Hart broke into a run, heading for the door, and jumped over the figure lying there. He went into the shack fast, his teeth clenched and his gun ready for action.

TWO

In the split second when he darkened the doorway, Hart saw two figures inside the shack. One was a woman, and she was struggling with Gimp Alder, whom Hart recognized at a glance. Alder swung around when he heard Hart's feet on the threshold, reaching for his holstered pistol as he did so. Hart swung his Winchester one-handed, smacking the barrel across Alder's right elbow. The outlaw's pistol cleared leather, but was sent flying before it could be levelled.

Hart bored in, his left fist snaking out with all the power of his fast-moving body behind the blow. His hard knuckles cracked against Alder's chin and the outlaw uttered a cry of shock as he dropped heavily to the hard earth floor. Hart bent over the man and slammed his pistol barrel against Alder's left temple. Alder relaxed instantly, blood appearing on his head from the gash that opened at the point of impact.

The woman leaned back against the table. She was middle-aged, small, black-haired. Her face was chalky white. She gazed at Hart with wide brown eyes that barely registered her surroundings. Hart straight-

20

ened, breathing heavily. He glanced around the shack, saw a length of rope coiled on a hook in the back wall, and fetched it. He bound Alder's wrists behind his back, and then stood up. Alder was regaining his senses.

Hart went to the man lying in the doorway. Blood had spread through the fabric of his shirt. He was dead. Hart went outside and crossed to the boy, who was dead with a bullet between his shoulder blades. The youngster was about fifteen years old. Hart fetched his horse and put it in the byre with the cow, unsaddling the animal, aware that he had a grim chore to perform. The dead needed burying.

He returned to the shack. Alder was lying on his left side. His eyes were closed, but Hart knew he was conscious. The woman had not moved. She sat on the edge of the table, lost in the misery of her grief. Hart crossed to her, grasped her shoulders and shook her gently.

'I'm Mike Hart, Texas Ranger,' he said gently. 'This man is Gimp Alder, an outlaw. What's your name?'

'Jane Garrett. Is Jim dead, and Billy?'

'They're both dead. I'm sorry. Do you want them buried out back?'

'This is our home. There's no place else I could take them where they'd rest easy.' She began to cry softly, burying her face in her work-worn hands.

'I'll attend to the chore.' Hart was at a loss for words and turned to the outlaw.

He grasped Alder, pulled the man upright, and then forced him out of the shack. Alder remained silent as Hart untied him, but his eyes narrowed when Hart drew his pistol and jabbed him in the belly with the muzzle.

'You'll find a spade in the barn, I reckon. You did the killing so you can do the burying.'

'Leave 'em for the buzzards,' Alder snarled.

Hart struck hard with his left fist, digging his knuckles into Alder's stomach. The outlaw fell to his knees. He looked up at Hart, his face contorted with hatred.

'You got the better of me at the moment,' he rasped, 'but it's a long way to the nearest jail.'

'I was ordered to bring you in dead or alive,' Hart said harshly. 'It don't matter none to me how you travel. Get up, fetch a spade, and then start digging.'

He dragged the outlaw to his feet. Alder lashed out. Hart expected resistance and took the blow on his left shoulder. He crashed the barrel of his pistol against Alder's left cheekbone. The outlaw fell as if he had been pole-axed, and more blood showed on his face. Hart holstered his pistol and dragged Alder to his feet.

'We may as well settle this now,' Hart said. 'You'll never accept that you can't get the better of me, so get up, make your play, and I'll batter the message through your thick skull. Then you can get to work digging the graves.'

Alder surged to his feet and came in swinging. Hart covered up, taking the blows on his arms, blocking and parrying. Alder expected him to give ground but Hart stood firm, and slammed two punches in quick succession into the outlaw's body. Alder wilted, and Hart hit him on the chin with a solid right-hand punch. Alder went down and stayed down. He looked up at Hart, shoulders heaving, his breath rasping in his throat.

'Had enough?' Hart demanded. 'There's plenty more of that, if you want it.'

Alder came up off the ground fast and walked into a right uppercut. He staggered, almost fell, and then the fight oozed out of him. His shoulders slumped and he turned towards the barn, feet dragging in the dust as he went to get a spade. Hart followed at a distance, ready for the outlaw's next attempt to overpower him.

'You killed a man this morning at the stream you passed,' Hart said.

Alder paused and looked round, surprise showing on his battered face. His left eye was swelling – already just a slit in the bruise that was developing around it. He shook his head.

'What are you trying to pull?' he demanded. 'I ain't seen a soul anywhere until I rode in here.'

'What about Grat Kane's place? You stopped off there for grub and coffee.'

'Did they tell you that?'

'Was it supposed to be a secret?' Hart smiled. 'I've been following your tracks for a couple of weeks. I saw the spot where you left your horse by the stream and the place where you hunkered down with your rifle. When someone showed up you shot him while he was taking a drink. It bore the stamp of your work – cold-blooded murder. Don't deny it. I saw the tracks of your horse back from the stream, and picked up the cartridge case you ejected from your Winchester after killing Luke Warner. No one else was around there, or had been in more than a week. You left tracks, and I read your actions from them.'

'Why would I have waited around in the hope that someone might show? I'll bet there ain't more than two men pass that stream inside of a month. I never did half the crimes they've tied to my name. You give me a good reason why I would do such a thing and I'll confess to it.' Alder grinned crookedly. 'We both know you're lying. I checked out the stream and found where the ambusher waited. I saw his tracks heading off, and I know you did the same. You know I didn't kill that guy so don't try to pin it on me.'

'What happened here? Did you have a good reason for killing Garrett and his son in cold blood? I got here just too late to stop you shooting the boy in the back. He didn't have a gun, and was running away at the time. What was your reason for that?'

'The man rubbed me up the wrong way. I stopped to water my horse and he wouldn't let me dismount. He was pointing a rifle at me. Something had fired him up, and I wasn't taking any chances. Mebbe he took me for someone else. They got trouble on this range, but I ain't a part of it. So he got the wrong idea about me, and I had to kill him.'

'You shot your horse before you reached this place,' Hart said.

Alder shook his head. 'Nope. I came in here for water, and then decided to lay for you and started along my back trail. My horse put a foot in a gopher hole and broke its blamed leg.'

24

'You mentioned trouble in these parts.'

Alder shrugged. His eyes were filled with wicked-ness.

'It ain't none of my business. I heard about it when I rode into K Bar. Grat Kane offered me money to kill one of his neighbours. They got trouble over water.'

'Who did Kane want killed?'

Alder grinned. 'Why don't you ask him? See how far you'll get with a man like him.'

Hart backed out of the barn as Alder emerged with a long-handled spade. He stayed out of arm's length and escorted Alder to the rear of the shack, pointing out where two graves should be dug. He stayed well clear as Alder began to dig. It took the outlaw two hours to get down to the depth required, and then Hart escorted Alder around to the front of the shack.

Mrs Garrett had prepared her husband and her son for burial, and Hart stood by while Alder carried first the man and then the boy around the shack to their last resting place. Mrs Garrett fetched a Bible from the shack and read from it, her voice breaking several times before she finished the simple service. When she retired into the shack afterwards, Hart watched Alder fill in the graves.

'What happens now?' Alder demanded as he threw himself down on the ground after tamping down the fresh earth on the graves.

'We head for the nearest town, so haul yourself up and let's get moving.'

'Give me a break. I'm beat right now from all that digging. Anyway, I ain't got a horse to ride. Mine's dead, remember?'

'So you can walk. On your feet, Alder.'

The outlaw arose and walked around the shack to the door. Hart called Mrs Garrett and she emerged from the ramshackle little building. Her dull gaze fixed itself upon Alder like a hungry dog spotting a piece of meat.

'What are you going to do with him?' she demanded. 'Shooting is too good for him.'

'I'll take him into Mesquite and hand him over to the local law. He'll stand trial for what he did here, and no doubt they'll hang him for it. What are you going to do? You shouldn't stay here alone.'

'I won't be alone. My husband and my son are here.'

'You can't run this place by yourself,' Hart protested.

'I'll manage. I'll hire help if it gets too much for me. There's a mule in the pasture out back. You can use it to take that killer into town. The sooner you get him there the sooner they'll hang him. If you follow the trail over there it'll take you right into Mesquite. You can tell the law I'll be riding in later to make a statement about what happened here, and to watch the hanging.'

'Thanks.' Hart turned away, aware that there was nothing he could do to help her.

Alder caught the mule under Hart's direction, put a halter on it, and mounted without protest. Hart stepped up into his saddle and they departed.

There was a faint trail leading off to the north-east and Hart urged Alder along it as fast as the mule would travel. Alder seemed to sink into depression, for he remained silent for the most part, his battered features showing despair. The long hours of the afternoon slipped away, and the evening was well advanced, with shadows crawling into the low places, when they eventually reached Mesquite.

Hart looked around with interest as they traversed the main street. He was tired, hungry and thirsty, but looked for the law office.

'Let's get a drink in that saloon before you turn me in,' Alder said. 'I'm parched right through to the spine.'

Hart shook his head. 'Your drinking days are over. The law office is along there. Get moving. I've had enough of your company. I'll be glad to see the back of you.'

They reined in at the hitching-rail in front of the office, and Hart drew his pistol as he dismounted. Alder turned swiftly the instant his feet touched the ground and launched himself at Hart in a last desperate attempt to gain the upper hand. He pulled up short at the sight of Hart's gun covering him and backed off, grinning ruefully.

A man was seated on a chair on the sidewalk in front of the office, almost invisible in the thickening shadows. Hart saw a law badge on the man's shirt front as he stood up.

'Say, that's Gimp Alder!' the man exclaimed. 'I'm Deputy Lew Seifert. Al Denton was in here earlier with the body of Luke Warner. He said a Ranger was trailing Alder. You must be Mike Hart. Where did you catch up with this killer?'

'I'm Hart. Let's get Alder behind bars and I'll make a report.'

Seifert led the way into his office. Hart stood with the muzzle of his gun jammed against Alder's spine until the deputy lit a lamp on his desk. Alder was searched and his personal belongings removed. Seifert picked up a bunch of keys and led the way into the cell block. Hart sighed in relief when a cell door clanged on Alder and a key grated metallically in the lock.

Back in the office, Hart related the incidents that had occurred since he found the body of Luke Warner in the stream. Seifert was shocked by the news that Jim Garrett and his son had been shot down in cold blood. He paced the office restlessly.

'I've been expecting trouble to flare around here.' Seifert was tall and lean, a man of around forty-five who seemed to be a good type, quietly confident. 'I sent a message to Captain Buckbee at Ranger head-quarters as you requested. Now you'll have to send him another one. Alder killed a Ranger last year, didn't he? There's a pile of dough on his head. He's wanted, dead or alive.'

'That's a fact, but his killing days are over now. Mrs Garrett will be coming in to make a statement about what happened to her husband and son. It's a pity Alder can only die once for his crimes. Have you got plenty of help around here? You'll need to be on your toes every minute you've got Alder. He escaped from prison once, and I've lost count of the number of times he's been captured and then escaped.'

Seifert grinned. 'He ain't likely to get away from

28

here. Will you be sticking around for a few days?'

'I'll have to wait for new orders to come for me. Apart from that, I need to rest up. I'll check with you later. Right now I need to take care of my horse, and then myself.'

Seifert walked to the street with Hart, and called to a youngster who was passing by.

'Johnny, show the Ranger to the telegraph office, will you?'

'Sure thing. Did you get Gimp Alder, Ranger?'

'News travels fast around here.' Seifert grinned at Hart. 'Yeah, we got Alder behind bars. Make yourself useful to the Ranger, Johnny, and afterwards you can come back here and I'll let you take a look at a real live outlaw.'

The youngster, aged about twelve years, agreed eagerly, and chatted to Hart, who hardly heard what he said. They visited the telegraph office, and Hart wired Captain Buckbee. He arranged for any reply to be delivered to him at the hotel. Then they went on to the livery barn, and Hart attended to his horse.

'I'm going back to the law office,' Johnny said as they left the stable.

Hart paused at the batwings of the saloon and peered inside.

'I wanta get a good look at Gimp Alder,' the boy continued. 'Did you have much trouble catching him?'

'Not much. Thanks for your help.' Hart smiled. 'Don't get too close to Alder. He's a mad dog. He might try to bite you.'

The youngster departed, grinning, and Hart

pushed through the batwings, feeling parched down to his boots. His tongue seemed like a piece of rawhide and his throat was lined with dust. He paused on the threshold, his weight making the sawdusted boards creak as he looked around. He became aware instantly of a powerful tension filling the big room.

A fair-sized crowd was present, drinking and gambling, and it seemed to be split into two factions. Voices were harsh, not exactly arguing but uttering loud opinions. A sense of menace laced the smoke-laden atmosphere, and Hart recognized it instantly, accustomed as he was to facing trouble. He became aware that, as he walked to the bar, silence fell over the saloon, while a dozen pairs of keen eyes focused on him.

He cuffed back his Stetson, revealing a shock of black hair, and hooked a heel over the brass rail that ran the length of the long bar. A barkeep, down at the far end of the room where a group of men had been talking the loudest until Hart's appearance, came reluctantly to serve him.

'Beer,' Hart told him, and threw a silver dollar on the smooth bar-top.

He glanced around the saloon again. There was a large picture of a reclining nude behind the bar. Oil-lamps threw a harsh glare over the assembled men, and there was a mixture of range-clad men and townsmen. Two middle-aged men, seated at a small table apart from the general throng, were dressed in broadcloth store suits – obviously professional men. Half-way along the bar, and standing alone in a small cleared space, was a tall, raw-boned man who was wearing black range-garb and crossed cartridge belts laden with twin six-shooters.

Hart sensed the tension as he picked up his glass of foaming beer. He almost emptied it before wiping his lips on the back of his left hand, noting that the barkeep was gazing at him.

'You sure needed that drink,' said the barkeep. 'Ridden a far piece today, huh?'

'Yeah.' Hart drained his glass and pushed it towards the man. 'Gimme another.'

The barkeep obliged. 'Al Denton was in here earlier,' he remarked. 'Said he found Luke Warner dead this morning, and met a Texas Ranger who was trailing Gimp Alder, the outlaw.'

'I wouldn't know a Ranger if I saw one,' Hart said, 'I never heard of Luke Warner, and who is Gimp Alder?'

'It's about time we saw some real law in Mesquite,' called one of the two professional men. 'I'm Doc Wesley, stranger, and I'm the man who has to patch up those individuals who get caught up in the trouble hereabouts. We heard there is a Ranger in the county, and opinions are divided about what he should do while he's here.'

'Being a stranger, I don't know a thing about what's going on around here,' Hart replied.

He drank his second glass of beer and began to feel almost normal inside. He was about to leave when the batwings were thrust open and a young man appeared on the threshold to gaze around blearily. He was unsteady on his feet as he checked out the men in the saloon, his right hand close to the butt of the pistol holstered on his hip. Aggression was plain in his face, and he looked primed for trouble.

'I'm looking for Pete Downey,' he announced belligerently. 'Has he been around?'

'You should be looking for your bed, Charlie, to sleep it off,' Doc Wesley said acidly. 'If you meet up with Pete tonight I'll have to patch up one or the other of you.'

'I don't need any advice from you, Doc. Just point me in the direction of Pete Downey. Him and me have something to settle.'

'Why don't you do like the doc says?' a harsh voice interrupted. 'You're making a nuisance of yourself, Shaw. Get the hell out and stop trying to act like a man.'

Hart looked along the bar and saw the two-gun man talking. He was standing with his back to the bar, his left elbow resting lightly upon it, his right hand hanging down by his side. Big and fair-haired, he looked to be around thirty-five, businesslike and capable. There was something in his manner which warned Hart that he was ready to take advantage of the situation.

Charlie Shaw straightened at the sound of the gunman's voice, his manner changing imperceptibly. He suddenly didn't seem to be as drunk as he had appeared.

'Why don't you keep your nose out of my business, Dexter,' he rapped. 'We all know you draw pay from Grat Kane, and no one is gonna swallow your bait. If you wanta push trouble between HR and K Bar then you're gonna have to murder one of us to set the ball rolling. But you won't come out into the open to do that, will you? You and the rest like you prefer to shoot from cover.'

'Like someone did to Luke Warner this morning, huh?' Dexter laughed harshly. 'It looks to me that HR are more at home shooting from cover. Who do you figure killed Warner? He was K Bar's foreman, so its stands to reason he was knocked off by one of Henry Reed's bunch.'

'I wouldn't put it past K Bar to shoot one of their own and blame it on HR.' Shaw took a step forward, his hand moving closer to his holstered gun, and demanded belligerently: 'Do you think we're scared of you at HR?'

'You can prove the rights of that right now.' Dexter stepped away from the bar, and there was general movement as those present moved quickly to get out of the line of fire. 'OK, Shaw, go to it. I'm a mite tired of hearing you squeaking around town. Put up or shut up.'

Hart took one pace away from the bar, which put him beside Charlie Shaw and facing towards Dexter. He reached out with his left hand and grasped Shaw's right wrist.

'It looks like this little show is getting out of hand,' Hart said mildly. 'Just hold your horses, both of you, while I do some explaining.' He lifted his right hand and tweaked his leather vest aside to reveal his Ranger badge, and a muttering surged through the saloon. 'I'm the Ranger you've heard about. I arrested Gimp Alder this afternoon and he's behind bars right now. I came in here to relax before going for my supper, and I sure don't want to spoil my appetite by witnessing a shoot-out. So cool off, both of you.'

Shaw tried vainly to pull his gun hand from Hart's grasp, but he was like a boy in the big Ranger's grip.

'Stand still,' Hart rasped. 'I'm trying to save you from getting yourself killed.'

'Turn him loose, Ranger,' Dexter urged. 'It's about time someone shut Shaw's mouth, and it looks like it's down to me.'

'I'm not asking you to pull in your horns,' Hart said. 'I'm telling you.'

Dexter straightened from the bar, his expression becoming inscrutable, but a flame gleamed in his eyes.

'No one tells me what to do,' he snapped.

Hart pulled his gun so fast that Dexter was still lifting his hands to his gun butts when the Ranger's big pistol levelled at him. He found himself looking into the black muzzle gaping menacingly at him and stopped all movement.

'I was hoping we could settle this without gun smoke,' Hart said mildly. 'But if that's the way you want it then I'll holster my gun and we'll start again. You call it.'

Dexter relaxed instantly, smiling, but his face was pale, his lips compressed. He shook his head.

'I don't want trouble with the law,' he said calmly. 'There'll always be another time for Charlie Shaw. You do it your way, Ranger.'

Hart turned to Shaw, who was still trying to get

loose from the grip on his wrist. Hart released the youngster, holstering his gun as he did so.

'Come with me, Shaw,' he said. 'I need to know what's going on around here, and you look like you might have plenty to say.'

'The hell I will!' Shaw backed off, reaching for his gun.

Hart palmed his pistol in a flash and slammed the barrel against Shaw's right temple. The youngster uttered a groan and collapsed. Hart shook his head. He had hoped to handle the situation the easy way. Now his supper would have to wait.

THREE

Hart bent over Charlie Shaw and took the young-ster's pistol from its holster. As he straightened, the batwings were thrust open and Seifert, the deputy, entered the saloon. He stopped short when he saw Hart and the unconscious Shaw.

'Trouble?' he demanded, glancing around the saloon.

'Nothing I can't handle,' Hart replied. 'You better stick Shaw behind bars until he's cooled down. I didn't want to step in, but somebody would have been killed if I hadn't.'

Seifert looked around again, and nodded.

'Dexter, were you mixed up in this?

'Shaw came in looking for trouble.' Dexter said. 'When he saw me he started to push it. The Ranger can tell you.'

Seifert bent over Shaw, grasped a shoulder and shook him vigorously. Shaw was groaning; his eyelids flickering.

'Come on, Charlie, wake up,' Seifert said. 'You'll have plenty chance to sleep in jail.'

Hart heard the sound of hoofs approaching in the

street and turned to face the batwings. Loud voices spoke outside, and then boots pounded the sidewalk. Two men pushed through the batwings and paused on the threshold. One was tall and powerfully built, in his thirties, hawk-faced and tough-looking. He was well dressed, and wore a pistol in a low slung holster in the fashion of a gunman. The other was twenty years older than his companion, and possibly bigger, but running into middle-aged bulk. The gun he was wearing was high on his gun belt on the left, butt forward to facilitate a cross-draw.

'What in hell is going on here?' demanded the older man. 'That's Charlie on the floor. What happened, Lew? Has there been a shooting?'

'It stopped short of that, Henry, thanks to the Ranger here. He stopped Charlie making a fool of himself. What was Charlie doing in town in the middle of the week, anyway? Can't you keep him out at HR? He's a nuisance around here on Saturdays, and we can do without him in between.'

'I sent him in this morning to collect the ranch mail.' Henry Reed was looking at Hart as he spoke. 'I came into town because Al Denton dropped by to tell me about Luke Warner getting dry-gulched. He said he saw a Ranger who thought the outlaw, Gimp Alder, killed Warner. That was you, huh?' His grey eyes were narrowed, filled with a brightness that told Hart a great deal about the man. 'Did you get that outlaw?'

'He's in jail now. I'm Mike Hart. I looked around the area where the shooting occurred and saw the tracks of Alder's horse, and spotted a second set that belonged to the ambusher. Alder didn't kill Warner.'

'Glad to know you, Hart. I'm Henry Reed. I own HR. Are you here to look into our trouble?'

'At the moment I'm between jobs, waiting for orders,' Hart said.

'I was in touch with Captain Buckbee,' Reed went on. 'He said he'd send a man to look around.' He indicated the man at his side. 'This is Flash Johnson, my foreman. He can tell you what's going on around here better than me.'

'Let's go to the law office,' Hart suggested. 'We can talk there.'

Seifert propelled Charlie Shaw towards the batwings, but the youngster was reluctant to accompany him and began to struggle.

'Charlie, behave,' Reed said. 'Go along with Lew.'

'I ain't done a damn thing wrong,' Shaw protested. 'I was looking for Pete Downey, that's all. Ginny told me he insulted her last Saturday, and I was gonna teach him some manners.'

'You were ready to fight anyone who would take you on,' Hart said. 'You should be locked up for your own protection.'

'The hell you say!' Shaw protested.

Seifert manhandled Shaw through the batwings and Henry Reed followed closely. Hart turned to follow but Johnson glanced around the long room, and smiled when he saw Dexter along the bar. He dropped his hand to the butt of his gun and eased the weapon in its holster.

'I might have known you were in here, Dexter,' he said. 'Still trying to cause trouble for my outfit, huh?

One of these days you'll make a stand against me, and I'm waiting on that.'

'Any time you feel lucky you only got to say,' Dexter replied.

Johnson turned to depart and Hart followed the foreman out to the sidewalk. They walked towards the jail.

'So you found Luke Warner,' Johnson mused. 'Was there any sign of what happened? Al Denton said Warner was shot in the back. That's the helluva thing to happen. Everyone will be thinking someone from HR did it. Apart from that, Warner was an all-right guy. He didn't seem to go along with the bad stuff his outfit was pulling. I'll never know why Grat Kane employed him. He knew his job, but didn't hold with violence, and that sure ain't Kane's way. He's a mad dog, and so is his son Wiley.'

'What is the trouble around here,' Hart asked.

'I can tell you in one word – water. Grat Kane said he'll stop the water-flow at our boundary, and if he does that our cows will die of thirst. We rely on that stream. Without it the few sinks and wells we got won't support half our stock. It surely means trouble when someone talks of stopping the water-flow.'

'The stream crosses Kane's range before it gets to HR?' Hart queried. He realized the trouble was most serious. Water was the essence of life to a cattleman.

'You got it. And you can bet that if Kane is talking about stopping our water then he'll do it when he's good and ready.'

'There's a law against damming natural water-courses,' Hart observed.

'Kane wouldn't let that stop him.'

'The law would stop him. Has anyone spoken to Kane about the rumour?'

'We've bent over backwards to get the law to act – Seifert here on the spot, and Sheriff Moore around the county, but it seems Kane can get away with anything. His outfit is always on the prod. You heard what Charlie said. Pete Downey insulted Ginny Reed last Saturday, and if you hadn't been here to stop him then the war would have started tonight. If I'd heard first what Downey did to Ginny I'd have come looking for him myself. But Dexter is always hanging around town, waiting for the chance to cut loose at anyone riding for HR.'

Hart remained silent, his thoughts deep. Water was the life-blood of cattle-ranching, and any threat to the supply had to be treated seriously. The friction between K Bar and HR was bad enough to give concern, and Hart wondered what lay behind it. To his way of thinking there had to be more than the mere threat to cut off the water.

They entered the law office to find Charlie Shaw lying unconscious on the floor. Henry Reed was looking angry. Seifert was smiling.

'Charlie doesn't want to spend the night in jail,' Seifert said.

'There's no need to get that rough with him.' Reed said sharply.

'Putting him out quickly is the easiest way of handling a hot-head like him,' Seifert retorted. 'He'll go quietly now. Watch him, Hart, while I unlock a cell. I'll turn him loose in the morning, Henry. He should be sobered up by then. I'll send him out of town first thing and set him on the trail to HR.'

Seifert went into the cell block, jingling a bunch of keys. Hart listened to the conversation that passed between Reed and Johnson, certain now that the situation was grave. Reed did not seem to be the type to cause trouble, but he advised his foreman to play it tough in future against K Bar.

'You know that ain't the way to handle it, boss,' Johnson protested. 'It's just what Kane is waiting for, what he's been angling for these past months. Look at the size of his crew. Half of them are gunnies. If he turned them loose on us we'd be hard put to survive.'

'I know you're right, Flash, but how much are we expected to swallow? The whole business has taken a turn for the worse. Who in hell shot Luke Warner in the back? None of our men was off the ranch, and I don't reckon any of them could have slipped away unnoticed. Who would know Warner was riding into town at that time in the morning, anyway?'

Johnson shook his head. 'All we do know is that the K Bar outfit crosses the stream at that point to get to town, so it would be easy for a killer to plan his move. I'm certain it wasn't anyone on our payroll, but I'm not so sure that a third party didn't do it just to throw the blame on us.'

'That's the helluva note, if you're right, Flash,' Reed mused. 'But it is something to think about.' He glanced at the alert Hart. 'I hope Captain Buckbee keeps his word about sending a Ranger in here. We could sure do with a good lawman to look into this business.'

'I'm on the spot,' Hart said, 'so it's likely I'll get the chore. I'll question Alder again in the morning, and put pressure on him. He might have seen something. What can you tell me about the trouble you've been getting? It might set me in the right direction, if I'm elected to handle it.'

'Whoever is back of it is playing his cards mighty close to his vest.' Reed shook his head. 'Like Flash says, apart from the obvious friction between K Bar and us, there seems to be a third party at work in the background, stirring the trouble whenever it cools off. I'm keeping a tight rein on my crew, but they're only human. Take Charlie Shaw. He worships the ground my daughter Ginny walks on, and when he heard she'd been insulted it was natural for him to go for Downey. I'm tempted to look up Downey myself and horsewhip him to teach him a lesson.'

Seifert came out of the cell block and Hart helped him carry the unconscious Shaw into a cell. Seifert heaved a long sigh when he locked the cell door.

'There's a load of trouble coming up because of Kane's attitude to HR,' he said thoughtfully. 'I got no idea what started it, but Kane has a son, Wiley, who is sweet on Ginnie Reed. She detests him, and I ain't surprised. Wiley ain't well up on social niceties, nor he ain't very presentable, and he ain't welcomed anywhere he alights. I had to warn him off from making a play for Ginny, and I think that fact alone started the friction between the two spreads. Wiley ain't the type to heed advice, and I reckon he's been pushing things on the quiet.'

Hart nodded. 'I have a hunch this business will be

tossed into my lap when I hear from Captain Buckbee, so I'll keep an open mind until I know for sure. I reckon it's time I paid some attention to my needs. I want to get some food before the town closes down for the night.'

'I'll walk with you to the eating-house along the street. If they have finished cooking for the day they'll always oblige anyone connected with the law. Rufus Hannon owns the place. He was a deputy here until he opened his business.'

'OK.' Hart grinned. He was thinking that Lew Seifert was a decent lawman, so why wasn't he getting on top of the trouble?

They went back into the office. Henry Reed was already on his way to the street door, but paused to address Seifert.

'So you'll turn Charlie loose first thing in the morning, huh?'

'Yeah. He should be sober enough then to be able to curb his recklessness. If he's not more careful, Henry, you'll be planting him on Boot Hill before long.'

Reed shrugged and departed. Flash Johnson glanced at Hart as he left the office.

'I hope you get the job of looking into this trouble,' he said, 'and the first place you want to start nosing around is K Bar.'

Hart nodded. He turned to Seifert.

'What's your opinion of what is going on?' he asked.

'I don't know a blamed thing.' Seifert shook his head.

'You've been on the spot the whole time, and will have been watching points.'

'Your guess is as good as mine. I do the best I can, but I got no idea what's happening. Trouble is certainly spreading. Take this business with Charlie Shaw. It ain't gonna blow over. Charlie is gonna keep pushing until Trig Dexter or Wiley Kane kills him. Charlie won't have a chance against either of them, and he knows it, but that won't stop him going off half-cocked.'

They left the office and walked along the street. The eating-house was about to close, but Hart managed to get a meal, and Seifert left him to eat it.

Later, Hart went back to the saloon. A dozen men were still present, but Dexter was no longer around. Hart had a beer, and was beginning to think of calling it a day when the batwings were thrust open and a big man stepped into the saloon. For a moment, Hart thought it was Grat Kane. Then he noticed differences between the two men. The newcomer was half Grat's age and, although massively built, he was not as large as the K Bar rancher. So this had to be Wiley Kane, Grat's son.

Wiley was dressed in outsize range clothes. His dull red shirt was straining at the seams. His arms were huge, his fleshy hands bigger than anything Hart had ever seen on a man. He stood at least six inches over six feet, and his progress from the batwings to the bar reminded Hart of a rampaging steer. He thrust himself between two townsmen, who quickly made themselves scarce, and slammed a ponderous hand on the bar top with a slap that shook it.

'Gime three fingers of rye and a beer chaser,' he rapped in a hoarse voice. 'And make it quick, Barney, or I'll separate you from your feet.'

The barkeep obeyed hastily, slopping beer on the bar, his expression showing mingled respect and fear.

'Leave the bottle,' Wiley rasped. 'Where's Charlie Shaw? I heard he was out looking for K Bar men. When I catch up with him I'm gonna teach him a lesson.'

'Charlie's in the jug, Wiley,' the barkeep said. 'He got on the wrong side of the Ranger.'

'Ranger? What Ranger?'

'He's the stranger along there to your left.' The barkeep retired to the far end of the bar and busied himself cleaning glasses.

Wiley looked around until his gaze fastened on Hart.

'Are you the Texas Ranger?' he bellowed.

'Yeah. What's on your mind?'

'Have a drink with me.'

'No thanks. I'm about to turn in for the day.'

'You found Luke Warner dead this morning, huh?'

'That's right.'

'I'll bet there was some stinking HR rider bending over him.'

'There was no one around when I found him.'

'You won't have to look far for the killer. He'll be a polecat riding for HR, and that's a fact. Sure you won't have a drink with me?'

'No thanks.'

'If you refuse me I'll have a mind to pour it down your throat. What would you think of that?'

'I'd think it was a stupid thing to get shot for.'

Wiley Kane laughed raucously, and the sound reminded Hart of a bull moose sounding off. Kane refilled his glass with rye and then emptied it with a single gulp.

'You think I'm only joshing, huh?'

'No one but a fool would lock horns with a Ranger,' Hart replied. 'I assumed you were joking, but you better know that I never joke.'

Wiley remained silent, his amusement fading. His dark eyes looked like those of a wild hog. There was no human animation in their depths, only a dangerous glitter. The silence in the big room seemed to stretch almost to breaking-point. Hart remained motionless, poised for trouble, and saw Wiley's attitude changing with the thoughts filtering through his mind.

'What kind of men are the Rangers taking these days? You're talking of shooting a man who is only joshing.'

'Joking is OK. It's when you get beyond that the shooting would start.' Hart smiled. 'You look like a man who doesn't know when to stop.'

Kane turned to face Hart, his right hand stationary at belt-level. He was not wearing a gun belt and holster but Hart could see the butt of a pistol protruding from his waistband. Kane grinned widely.

'I reckon you're pushing it,' he said, and set his hand into motion, reaching for his pistol.

Hart moved the instant he saw the start of Kane's

draw. His pistol leapt into his hand, and the weapon was cocked before Kane could get into action. Kane paused, his gun, as yet uncocked, still pointing in the general direction of the floor. His grin widened slowly as he thrust the weapon back into his waistband and dropped his hand to his side.

'You're kind of nervy, ain't you, Ranger?' he said.

Hart shook his head. 'Nope. Just careful.'

'I was only joking.' Kane flexed his thick fingers.

'A man could get himself killed, trying jokes like that.' Hart motioned with his gun. 'Take your pistol out and throw it on the floor.'

'So you can't take a joke, huh?' Kane grasped the butt of his gun.

'Use your finger and thumb only or I'll drop you,' Hart warned.

Kane's expression changed. His eyes narrowed and his chest swelled as he drew a deep breath.

'Don't carry this too far, Ranger,' he warned. 'I ain't long on patience. In fact, I got an almighty short fuse.'

'Just do like I say or I'll snuff out your candle,' Hart replied. 'And do it slow.'

Kane took out his gun and threw it on the floor at Hart's feet.

'If you're carrying any other weapons, get rid of them now,' Hart said. 'You might have been joking, but I'm not. Step out of line and I'll drop you.'

Kane reached around to his back, pulled another pistol from his waistband, and tossed that in Hart's direction.

'Anything else?' Hart demanded.

'Nope. That's it.'

'So get outa here and head for the calaboose.' Hart smiled. 'You're gonna spend the night behind bars. It'll teach you that I ain't a joking man.'

'There ain't no call to go that far, Ranger. You're riling me, and that ain't good.'

'Don't make it worse for yourself by resisting. Turn around and start walking before I get impatient.'

Kane turned ponderously and strode towards the door. He almost took the batwings off their hinges as he shouldered through them, and the swing-doors crashed back behind him. Kane turned swiftly, moving surprisingly fast for such a big man. He came back through the batwings like a mad bull; his big hands lifted shoulder high, his fingers working spasmodically. His massive right foot was lifting to kick Hart. There was a wild light in his eyes and he was growling like a dog.

Hart was expecting resistance. Wiley Kane had all the earmarks of a man who would not be bested in anything. He sidestepped the massive figure and struck shrewdly with his pistol as Kane blundered by, catching him across his forehead with the long barrel. Kane dropped to his knees like a pole-axed steer before falling slowly on his face, his impact with the floor rattling the glasses on the bar.

'This man takes a lot of convincing about some things,' Hart said, shaking his head.

'You just made a bad enemy, Ranger,' the barkeep said. 'The minute Wiley gets his hands on a gun he'll come for you. You'll have to kill him to stop him.'

Hart bent over the big man and checked him out. Kane's eyes were blinking, and he was slobbering in the sawdust. Hart prodded him with the toe of his boot and got no immediate reaction.

'Come on, Kane. It's time to wake up. It was only a little tap on the head. I got the impression that you were tough, but I guess you fooled me. You ain't tough – you just smell strong.'

Kane snorted as he came back to full consciousness. He shook his head several times

'On your feet when you're ready,' Hart said, and moved back out of arm's length.

Kane's hat had fallen off his head and he reached out for it. There was blood oozing from a cut on his forehead. His eyes were filled with shock. He clamped his hat back on his head and levered himself up off the floor to stand swaying like a tree about to fall to a woodsman's axe.

'You better shoot me dead right on this spot, Ranger,' he mumbled. 'I'll sure as hell kill you the minute I'm able.'

'You'll never be able to do that. On your way, Kane. I reckon you know where the jail is. Let's get you a bed for the night. We'll take this up again in the morning. I've had enough for one day, so don't give me any more trouble.'

Kane turned and thrust his way through the batwings. Hart followed closely, ready for trouble, but Kane made no further attempt to resist. They went along the street to the jail, and Lew Seifert got the shock of his life when Wiley walked in on him with his hands in the air.

Hart, following closely on the heels of the big man, caught a glimpse of the slight figure of a girl with the deputy. He went forward quickly, suddenly alarmed, for Kane grabbed the girl and swung her around as if she were a doll. A long-bladed knife appeared in Kane's right hand and he pressed the cold steel against the girl's throat.

'Back off,' Kane rasped. 'You try anything and she'll bleed like a stuck pig.'

Hart moved back, his pistol down at his side. Kane held the girl with one hand, the other pressing the knife to her throat. Her feet were barely touching the floor. Kane backed to the door and eased out to the sidewalk, growling like a wild animal. Hart could have shot Kane in the head, but refrained because the girl would surely get hurt as the big man collapsed.

'Follow me and she gets it in the neck,' Kane warned hoarsely as he faded into the night.

Hart started to the door but paused when Seifert grasped his arm.

'That's Ginny Reed he's got,' the deputy said harshly. 'There'll be hell to pay over this. How'd you come to be bringing Kane in? What happened?'

'That doesn't matter right now,' Hart said sharply. 'We've got to pull that girl from Kane before he gets away.'

'She better be alive when Kane has finished with her.' Seifert's voice was filled with foreboding. 'If anything happens to that girl, the county will run red with blood.'

Hart departed swiftly, cursing himself for permitting Kane to turn the tables on him. The big man had a hostage, an innocent girl, and disaster loomed. It was a situation that had to be retrieved immediately.

FOUR

A scream echoed through the shadows along the street, grating on Hart's tautly stretched nerves. He stepped off the sidewalk and ran towards the sound, his feet muffled by thick dust, and Seifert followed closely. They could not see much in the darkness, and Hart carried his pistol with the muzzle pointing at the ground.

'I reckon he's making for the livery barn,' Seifert said. 'He better not harm that girl.'

Hart did not reply, saving his breath for running, and soon outstripped the deputy. He could see the yellow glare of a lantern hanging over the big open door of the barn at the end of the street, and Kane's massive figure showed briefly as the man entered the building, half-carrying Ginny Reed. Hart slowed and moved in silently, angling for the nearest front corner of the low building. Seifert arrived, entered the alley beside the stable, and hurried to the rear.

The rumble of Wiley Kane's voice reached Hart's ears as he eased forward. A lantern was burning inside the barn. Hart found a knot-hole in the wall and applied an eye to it. He saw Kane standing by the nearest stall, binding Ginny Reed's hands with the end of a lariat. He moved into the stall as Hart watched, and began to saddle a big black stallion.

Hart moved to the open doorway and risked a quick look inside. He saw Seifert entering by the back door. The deputy was looking grim. There was no easy way of tackling a man like Wiley Kane, and they both knew it, but Hart's concern was for the girl. He was afraid she might get hurt if shooting erupted.

He slipped in through the doorway, gun levelled. Ginny Reed spotted his movement and looked towards him. Hart motioned with his hand for her to drop to the ground, but she seemed scared out of her wits and did not move. Hart sneaked to his left to put the girl out of the line of fire. She was practically in the clear when Kane led his horse out of the stall and spotted him.

Kane bellowed furiously. He dropped his reins and made a lunge for the girl. Hart shouted a warning but the big man was deaf to everything. Hart threw up his gun and triggered a shot that blasted out the silence. The bullet struck Kane in the chest, high up on the right, almost in the shoulder. Kane cursed but did not even flinch. He grasped Ginny with his big left hand and reached over his right shoulder with his right hand. Lamplight gleamed on the long blade of a skinning-knife as he brought it into view.

Hart clenched his teeth and fired a snapshot, aiming for the man's right hand. The bullet passed the girl by a hair's breadth and struck Kane, who lost his grip on the knife, which went flying to the ground. Kane lifted the girl to use her as a shield.

Hart dashed forward, pistol swinging, and struck viciously at Kane's right wrist, which was dripping blood.

Kane let go of the girl and thrust her away. He turned on Hart like a wounded bear, his left hand lifting to make contact, his fingers clenching and unclenching convulsively. Hart ducked under the arm and straightened, using his head as a battering ram, and smashed his forehead against the bigger man's chin. He staggered at the solid contact but Kane merely shouted defiance and threw his right arm around Hart's neck.

Seifert arrived, swinging his pistol in a wide arc. He smashed the barrel against Kane's head. Hart kicked Kane in the right knee and the big man staggered, shouting at the top of his voice. He backed away like a moose at bay, shaking his head. Hart went in and back-handed him with his pistol, catching him across the mouth. Kane yelled again, spitting blood and broken teeth. His lower face was smeared with blood but he was not finished. He hurled himself sideways, intent on regaining his knife. Hart kicked him in the back of the right knee, then jabbed him in the side with his gun.

'Don't try it, Kane,' Hart warned. 'You'll be dead if you keep pushing.'

Kane ignored the warning and hurled himself to the ground, snatching up his knife. Seifert rushed in, gun swinging, and Hart stepped in close. Seifert struck first, catching the back of Kane's head even as the big man whirled, lifting the knife to continue his resistance. Seifert landed two blows on Kane's head and blood showed as Kane fell forward on his face and then relaxed inertly.

'I'd rather fight a bear than Wiley Kane any day,' Seifert remarked as he straightened. 'Keep an eye on him, Hart, while I check Ginny.'

Hart shook his head as he gazed down at the unconscious man-mountain. Kane was slobbering in the straw, raising dust with his heavy breathing. Hart holstered his gun and grasped Kane with both hands, heaving with all his strength to roll him over on to his back. He stepped back and looked around.

Seifert was untying Ginny, talking soothingly as he did so. The girl was badly shocked. Her taut face was pale, her eyes wide and glimmering with fright. She suddenly collapsed as if her legs had lost their strength. Seifert grasped her and eased her limp body against the boards of the nearest stall, leaning her in a sitting position.

'She'll be all right,' Seifert said. 'Watch Kane while I fetch the doctor. We sure had to hammer him. I hope we ain't killed him. I want him to stand trial for grabbing this gal. It's the first time I've had a good, solid charge against Wiley Kane.'

Hart went over to the girl as Seifert hurried off. He dropped to one knee beside her and grasped her hands, chafing them briskly to bring her back to her senses. It was the first chance he'd had of looking at her. Ginny Reed was attractive, tall and slim of figure. Her low-crowned hat had fallen from her head and was suspended at her back by its strap, allowing a mass of auburn hair to fall about her face. A low moan escaped her and her eyelids flickered as she regained consciousness.

'You're all right, Miss Reed,' Hart said softly.

She stiffened as the horror of her experience returned to her shocked mind, and grasped Hart's hands as she opened her eyes and looked around. She saw the inert figure of Wiley Kane lying a few yards away and uttered a low cry of fear.

'Is he dead?' she whispered.

'It'll take a lot more than we gave him to finish him off, I reckon.' Hart laughed harshly. 'He sure took some putting out. A smaller man would be dead, I reckon, but Kane will survive to give us a lot more trouble. Let's get you up on your feet.'

He took hold of her under the arms and eased her gently to her feet. She staggered and then leaned against the stall for support. Hart could feel her shivering. She was breathing heavily, fighting against shock.

'I hope you can keep this business from my father,' she said weakly. 'I fear to think of what would happen if he learns of it.'

'Did Kane hurt you? He handled you roughly.'

'I think I'm all right.' She smiled wanly. 'My ribs feel as if a horse fell on me. I don't think Wiley meant to hurt me. He was using me as a shield against you and Lew.' She paused and regarded Hart intently. 'You're a stranger. You must be the Ranger I heard about. Thank you for tackling Wiley. Some men would have had second thoughts about tangling with such a monster. He's a one-man stampede when he gets going, and I've seen six men trying unsuccessfully to stop him rampaging. His father is the only one who can control him.'

'I'm Mike Hart, and you're Ginny Reed.' Hart smiled. 'I'm glad this turned out to be nothing more than a bad fright for you. Like you said, I don't think Kane would have hurt you, but we couldn't take any chances. There's no telling how a man like him will turn when he's cornered. Can you stand alone now?'

'I think so.' She drew a deep breath and grasped the rail at her side.

'I'd better take a look at Kane.'

Hart crossed to the inert figure and dropped to one knee. Kane was still unconscious, and gave no sign of regaining his senses. His face showed the gory consequences of the gun-whipping he had sustained. There were cuts and bruises on his forehead and cheeks, and blood was dribbling from his slack mouth. The bullet he had taken had merely creased his right armpit.

Hart heaved a sigh and regained his feet. Seifert reappeared in the doorway of the barn at that moment. He was breathless.

'Doc will be along in a minute,' he said. 'How are you feeling now, Ginny?'

'I'm all right, although I feel as if I've been caught up in a stampede.'

'Like I was telling you before Kane went berserk,' Seifert said, 'we had to lock Charlie Shaw in a cell. He almost got in a gunfight with Trig Dexter when he went into the saloon looking for Pete Downey. If Hart hadn't been there, I guess Charlie would be dead now. He ain't in the same class as Dexter. What did Downey say to you that triggered Charlie off like that?'

'It wasn't much at all. I kept telling Charlie to forget about it, but you know him. He gets his feet moving in a certain direction and there ain't anything gonna stop him.'

Doc Wesley came in through the wide doorway, carrying a brown medical bag, and paused to look around. He was pushing sixty, and his years of doctoring patients in the wild country had stamped indelible marks on him. He was tall and thin, looked as if he didn't get enough to eat, and his eyes were tired-looking because his nights were regularly interrupted by the demands of his work. He shook his head at the sight of Wiley Kane stretched out on the ground.

'Are you all right, Ginny?' he asked, going to the girl's side.

'Yes, Doc. Wiley was a bit rough on me, and that's all.'

Wesley grunted and turned his attention to the unconscious Kane. They watched in silence while he bent over the man. The doctor straightened after a cursory examination.

'You really laid into him,' he observed. 'He looks like he's been trampled by his horse.'

'You know Wiley when he's aroused,' Seifert said harshly. 'It takes a runaway train to stop him. He had a knife he was keen on using.'

'You'd better get some help, put him on a door, or something, and bring him along to my place. I can't work on him in here. I'll expect you in a few minutes. Ginny, you'd better go back to HR and stay there until this trouble is over. It certainly looks like it's going to break now. Grat Kane will be on the warpath when he learns what's happened to Wiley, and I reckon your father will come out fighting when he gets the word that Wiley laid hands on you.'

'I have a room at the hotel,' she replied. 'I'll go back to the ranch in the morning.'

'I'll see you to the hotel.' Wesley took the girl's arm and led her away.

Seifert crossed to Kane's side and toed him gently. There was no response from the big man and Seifert grimaced. He dropped to one knee beside Kane and examined him closely, lifting an eyelid and then feeling for a pulse.

'We sure put it across him,' he mused, 'slamming him around the head like we did. But there ain't no other way of dealing with Wiley. He had that knife, and it sure looked to me like he would use it on Ginny if we didn't stand off. Stay with him while I rouse out some men to get him over to the doc's place.'

Hart nodded. Seifert departed, and Hart retrieved Kane's knife from where it lay in the straw. He heard footsteps outside the big door and turned, certain that Seifert could not be returning yet. Dexter, the K Bar gunman, appeared, and halted in shock at the sight of Wiley Kane stretched out on the ground. His right hand moved instinctively towards his hip, then stopped. He looked questioningly at Hart.

'Is he dead?' he asked.

Hart shook his head. 'No. He's out cold.'

'What happened to him?'

Hart explained and Dexter smiled.

'There'll be hell to pay over this,' he said. 'Grat Kane will go up in smoke when he hears about it.'

'You reckon he won't care that his son manhandled a girl?' Hart narrowed his eyes and his tone hardened. 'I ain't got the time of day for a man who would agree with what Wiley did here.'

'You got hold of the wrong end of the stick.' Dexter moved to Wiley's side and bent over him. He looked up sideways at Hart, smiling tensely. 'Grat is a God-fearing man, for all his wild ways, and he's got rigid principles. He'll probably take a bullwhip to Wiley when he gets the story. He's warned Wiley more than once to keep away from Ginny Reed.'

Hart nodded. 'What about the water problem that seems to be going on here? Is there truth in the rumour that Grat Kane plans to divert the stream north of HR?'

'I don't know anything about that. I have heard the rumour, but Grat ain't said a thing to me, and I'd be the first to know if he had that in mind. I reckon there's someone else around here who would like to see trouble blossom between K Bar and HR. You get on to whoever it is and you might avert a range war. Grat is powerful worked up about something, and Wiley is bent on the same hell-trail. I don't know what's setting fire to their tails, but there is smoke coming from both of them, and has been for some time.'

Hart nodded. 'You got any idea who might be interested in a war breaking out between your people and HR?'

'What makes you think I'd tell you if I knew?'

'Common sense. You wouldn't want to get caught up in fighting between the two outfits. If a third person is out to cause trouble between the ranches it would be in your interests to stop him.'

'Yeah, you're right. But I got no idea what's going on behind cover. If there is someone pushing for war then he's hiding his tracks pretty good.' Dexter moved away to collect his horse. 'I'm heading back to K Bar now. You want I should tell Grat about his boy?

'If you do it will save me a ride out to the ranch. I reckon I'm gonna get this case tossed in my lap.' Hart nodded. 'Tell Grat to come on in soon as he can.'

Dexter nodded and saddled his bay. He touched his hat-brim with a forefinger as he departed.

Hart lifted a hand and stood watching the gunman ride out to disappear in the murk of the night. He checked Kane again, and shook his head when he found no sign of returning consciousness in the big man. Minutes later, voices sounded outside, and Seifert appeared, leading four men who were carrying a door between them. Wiley was lifted on to the door and borne away. Seifert grinned at Hart. He held out his hand for the knife Hart was holding.

'If that is Wiley's knife then I'll want it for evidence,' he said. 'I'm gonna have to charge him for the disturbance he caused.'

'I should get a wire in the morning,' Hart mused. 'If I draw this case then I'll need to take control quickly, before the situation gets out of hand. It looks to me that everything is balancing on the edge of action.'

'Sure. I'll see you in the morning.' Seifert turned to leave, easing Kane's knife into his waistband.

They left the stable together. Seifert went off along the street and Hart entered the hotel, where he signed for a room before going up to it. Minutes later he was asleep on the bed, and lay unmoving until morning. The sun peeping in at his window and playing upon his face awoke him, and he sat up to face the reality of a new day.

Hart cleaned his pistol before leaving the room, and then went down to the dining-room for breakfast. Afterwards he walked to the law office, but turned off impulsively at the door of the mercantile and entered the dark interior of the store. A tall, thin man appeared from a back room and gazed silently at him.

'Box of .45 shells,' Hart said, and paid for his purchase when it was placed in silence before him. 'Nice day outside,' he added as he departed, and grimaced when he received no reply.

Hart entered the law office and found Seifert already at his desk. The deputy grinned.

'Wiley came to in the night,' he said. 'He's sure got a thick skull. He's in a cell now. I've had words with him this morning. He reckons to kill you and me both when he straps on a gun again. But he'll cool down some by the time he gets free.'

'Has Grat Kane showed up yet? Dexter rode out to K Bar last night with the news about Wiley. I thought Grat would have showed up before now.'

'There's no telling which way he'll jump, ever. I think hell will be popping when Henry Reed learns

62

what Wiley did to Ginny. I sure know how he'll react.'

'Are you turning Charlie Shaw loose this morning?'

'I got no legal reason to hold him. I don't reckon to charge him with anything. That would kind of aggravate the situation.'

'I'll go along to the telegraph office to check for the wire I'm expecting.'

'I reckon you'll be stuck with this business.' Seifert nodded. 'And it looks like turning into a real jamboree. I'm gonna be busy getting at the truth of what happened to Luke Warner. His murder could be the lever that turns the unrest around here into all-out war.'

'What's the name of the storekeeper in the mercantile?' Hart asked.

'Ossie Payne. He's a real sour-face with a manner to match. Ossie's only son was shot dead outside the saloon about six months ago and we never caught his killer. I found out that he was seen in the company of a couple of K Bar's outfit before he died, but I couldn't prove anything. Ossie is taking Billy Payne's death badly. He ain't even got the time of day for anyone around town, and I don't reckon he'll change his attitude until he finds out exactly what happened to his boy.'

Hart nodded, left the office and walked along the street to the telegraph office, arriving there as the operator turned up to start his shift. There was a wire waiting for Hart, and he was not surprised, upon reading it, to learn that he had to start investigating the local trouble. Captain Buckbee also ordered that

Gimp Alder should stand trial for any crime he had committed in Blackthorn County before being sent back to the scene of his last known crime.

Hart sent an acknowledgement to headquarters and prepared to handle his assignment. He went back to the law office and acquainted Seifert with the news. They both entered the cell block, and Seifert remained in the background while Hart approached the cell where Wiley Kane was incarcerated. The big man was lying on the bunk on his back, hands behind his head. His eyes were open but he gave no sign of having seen Hart. He looked as if he had been in a fight with a grizzly bear. His face bore several bruises, swellings and cuts. His left eye was almost closed and greatly discoloured. Dried blood was smeared around his heavy face.

'How are you feeling this morning, Kane?' Hart queried.

'A lot better than you'll be feeling when I get out of here. I've got a big score to settle with you, Ranger.'

'How old are you?' Hart countered.

'He's thirty,' Seifert said when Kane remained silent.

'It sounds like he's ten years old,' Hart observed. 'A man wouldn't talk like that.'

Kane came off the bunk and hurled himself at the bars of the door, growling in rage.

'You won't feel so pleased with yourself when Pa comes riding into town with the outfit at his back. He'll take this place apart with his bare hands to get at you.'

'I hope he's got more sense than you,' Hart retorted, 'or he'll be in here with you.'

Kane cursed and reached through the bars with his right hand. His massive fingers seized hold of Hart's vest and twisted. The next instant he howled in pain and released his grip, for Hart had drawn his pistol speedily and struck Kane's wrist. The big man stepped back from the bars, massaging his wrist.

Hart returned his pistol to its holster and stepped in front of Alder's cell. The outlaw was seated on the edge of his bunk. His fleshy face was expressionless and he regarded Hart with the wildness of a trapped animal.

'What have you got to say for yourself this morning, Alder?' Hart enquired.

'I didn't kill that guy Warner yesterday. You ain't gonna get away with pinning that on me. What's the big idea? Ain't I got enough charges against me already without you framing me with some more?'

'I know you didn't do it.' Hart nodded. 'I found the tracks of another horse at the scene. I know the prints of your mount, and they didn't lead in to the murder scene.'

'You said yesterday you thought I did it. What kind of a game are you playing?'

'I need to know if you're mixed up in the trouble they've got around here. You rode into K Bar, and Grat Kane seems to be in it up to his neck.'

'I stopped there for grub and no other reason.'

'I'll believe you this once. Have you committed any other crimes around here, apart from the killings at the Garrett place?'

'You know I ain't. You've been on my trail for weeks.'

Hart turned away. He went back into the law office and Seifert followed him.

'Like I told Alder,' Hart said, 'I saw prints of the killer's horse, and I'll know them again if I see them. They were heading towards town, and maybe that horse is around here right now. I'll go along to the stable to check, and if I'm lucky we might get the deadwood on the killer without too much trouble.'

'I'd go with you, but I got a lot to do at the moment. Keep me posted on what you find.'

'Sure.' Hart got half-way to the street door when a thought struck him and he paused, reaching into his breast pocket. He produced the used rifle cartridge he had picked up at the ambush spot and examined it closely. 'I found this by the stream. I reckon the bullet from it is the one that killed Luke Warner. Take a close look. The hammer of the rifle has struck the cartridge cap slightly off centre, and there's a big scratch down one side, likely made when it was ejected from the breech.'

Seifert took the case, studied it for a moment, and then nodded.

'So we got two bits of evidence. All we got to do is find the horse whose tracks you saw and arrest its rider, and match this cartridge case with the rifle that fired it. Looks like a Winchester 44.40 to me. I'll make a start checking long guns now.'

'And I'll look at the shoes of all the horses in town.'

Hart departed and went along the sidewalk

towards the livery barn with an easy stride, looking around at the town with interest. He was only yards from the big open door of the stable when a burst of shooting emanated from the building, blasting out the silence and hurling echoes across the town. He ran forward instinctively, and when he entered the barn his pistol was in his hand.

FIVE

Hart entered the barn and moved quickly to the left, flattening himself against the inside of the front wall, his pistol cocked and ready for action. Pungent gunsmoke was drifting through the gloomy interior. Two figures were lying motionless side by side in the walkway that led to the rear door. A noise over his head alerted Hart; he dived to his left and rolled on the hard floor to bring his gun to bear on the hayloft. Boots rustled through straw over his head, and then pounded furiously towards the rear before ceasing abruptly. Hart remained still, covering the area. Full silence came, filled with tension, and he drew a deep breath as he regained his feet, sensing that the unknown gunman had departed.

Gun ready, Hart stepped out into the open walkway, checking out what he could see of the hayloft. He turned his attention to the two still figures lying on the ground and went to them. Both men were dead. They were young, in their twenties; dressed as range hands. They had both been shot repeatedly in the back. Both were wearing pistols in holsters but neither had attempted to draw a weapon.

Hart looked at the loft again, and estimated that the killing shots had been fired from near the spot where the loft ladder was situated. He heard a noise out beyond the big front door, and turned in that direction as Lew Seifert appeared. The deputy saw Hart and came into the barn, holstering his gun.

'I feared the worst when I heard those shots and realized they came from here,' Seifert said.

'They were not fired at me.' Hart indicated the two dead men. 'Can you put names to these?'

Seifert expression hardened as he moved in. He looked down at the corpses for some moments, shaking his head in disbelief as he transferred his attention to Hart. Shock was showing plainly in his eyes.

'Jake Sarn and Blackie Thomas,' he said in a brittle tone. 'They rode for K Bar. What in hell is going on?'

'It's easy enough to work out. They were shot in the back by someone waiting up in the loft. I had almost reached the door when about six shots were fired in here. I came in at a run, but the killer was too fast for me. I heard his boots up there in the loft, and then there was silence. I don't think he's still up there. He wouldn't wanta hang around after a double killing.'

'I'll go up and take a look around.' Seifert hurried to the loft ladder. 'Cover me,' he called over his shoulder as he ascended.

Hart watched the gloomy space under the high roof. Seifert vanished from sight as he neared the rear of the loft, and then his voice floated down.

'There's an opening up here where they bring in

69

the hay and straw. Looks like our man escaped this way. He must have jumped down on to a stack of straw bales outside.'

Hart ascended the loft ladder as Seifert came back to him, and scrabbled around in the loose straw at the top of the ladder, searching for spent cartridge shells. He found two lying on the floor and picked them up. Seifert remained silent, watching intently as Hart examined them.

'Do you remember the marks on the spent shell I picked up at the stream where Luke Warner was killed?' Hart asked.

'Yeah. The hammer struck the cap off centre, and there was a deep scratch on the side of the shell.'

'These two were likely fired from the same rifle.' Hart handed one of the shells to Seifert. 'We'll need to get hold of the rifle that fired them to do tests, but it looks like the murder weapon is in town, and someone ain't through using it. The marks are too similar to be a coincidence. Have any K Bar men been killed before Warner was shot yesterday?'

'No.' Seifert shook his head. 'So what's triggered off this business? And why were these two men in town this early?'

'Could have been because Wiley Kane is behind bars,' Hart mused. 'I was expecting Grat Kane to show up, seeing that we have his son in jail.'

'Let's take a look out back.' Seifert moved impatiently. 'The killer jumped out of the loft on to a stack of straw bales. We better check this out before we look elsewhere.'

Hart nodded. They went to the rear of the barn.

The back lots were deserted. Hart went to the stack of baled straw under the loft doorway and walked around it, checking for footprints in the dust. There were plenty, but too muddled to unravel.

'Anyway, we know the rifle is in town,' Seifert mused. 'I reckon we'll have to make a house-to-house search and see if we can turn it up.'

Before they could go on, Hart heard the sound of rapidly approaching hoofs. The next instant, three riders rode through the barn from the front, and others came out of the alley at the side of the stable. Led by Grat Kane, they converged in front of Hart and Seifert and reined in. Dust billowed slowly around them as they sat motionless, gazing at the two law men.

'Got you dead to rights,' Grat Kane rumbled in his harsh voice. 'I've been waiting for you to show. You got some explaining to do, Seifert, so get to it and gimme the truth. You got my boy in jail, and you better have a good reason for putting him there.'

Hart looked around while Kane was speaking, and missed the face of Trig Dexter among the nine tough riders confronting them. None was holding a gun, but most of them had their hands close to their holsters.

'If you want an explanation about Wiley then put up your horse and come to the law office,' Seifert said. 'Your mob tactics won't work around here, Grat. We got a serious charge against Wiley, and he'll stay in jail until we can bring him to trial.'

'And come alone,' Hart added. 'The office ain't big enough for a group this size.'

71

Kane stepped down from his horse to confront them. He stood nearly a head taller than Hart, and looked as wide as the barn behind him. His bearded face was unlovely in the morning sun; his eyes filled with the wildness of a cornered buffalo.

'Ranger, you're a stranger here so I'll make an allowance for your ignorance. But I'll tell you just once, so mark my words good. When I speak, everyone jumps, if they know what's good for their health. I asked a plain question and I ain't coming along to no jail to get the answer. So tell me what happened in town last night that had to end with my boy being pistol-whipped and stuck in jail.'

Hart shrugged. He could tell by Kane's manner that the big man would not move from his attitude, so he explained the events leading up to Wiley Kane's violent arrest. Grat Kane heard him out in silence, his eyes narrowing as the details unfolded and, when Hart lapsed into silence, the big K Bar rancher slammed his right fist into his left palm.

'You expect me to believe that my boy would lay hands on a woman?' he snarled. 'Who concocted that story? The way I raised him, Wiley wouldn't harm no woman. You've made a big mistake, branding him with that lie.'

'That's how it was,' Hart said, 'and that's all you're gonna get right here. You want any proof then come along to the office, but come alone. You don't scare us with your outfit, so give up on the idea.'

'And before you commit yourself to any kind of action you'd better hear the latest,' Seifert said. 'Have you and your men just ridden into town?'

'We've been waiting outside town for you two to show on the street. When the Ranger went into the barn, we mounted up and came in for a reckoning.'

'Did you hear the rifle shots that were fired just before I went into the barn?' Hart asked.

'I said I heard shots, boss,' one of the riders said.

'Jake Sarn and Blackie Thomas,' Seifert said. 'What were they doing in town ahead of the rest of you?'

'I sent them in to watch for you and the Ranger,' Grat said. 'They wouldn't have gotten into any trouble. They're good, dependable men.'

'They found trouble,' Hart said. 'Both are dead, shot in the back. They're lying in the barn just as I found them.'

Shock hit Kane and his eyes widened. His lower jaw sagged, and then snapped shut.

'What are you giving me?' he snarled. 'If anything has happened to those two then this town will rue the day.'

'Cut out the threats and come and take a look,' Seifert invited, and entered the barn with Grat Kane following.

Hart accompanied them as they went to the bodies; and Kane uttered a hollow groan when he saw his two men.

'What in hell happened?' he demanded.

'We don't know yet, but the rifle that killed them was used yesterday to kill Luke Warner.' Seifert shook his head. 'Someone's got it in for K Bar, and he ain't wasting any time making his play.'

'How do you know about the rifle?' Kane asked.

'I'm not prepared to reveal evidence,' Hart replied. 'If you want us to catch this killer then move out from under our feet and let us get on with the job. Come along to the jail and talk to Wiley. But don't try to interfere with the processes of the law. You'll only make matters worse if you horn in.'

'I ain't about to leave my boy behind bars. If he did what you say he did then I'm gonna take him to task, and he sure won't forget his manners in future.'

'Tell your crew to get some coffee,' Seifert said. 'You don't need them along.'

'The hell you say! There's a killer around town who's taken to shooting up K Bar men, and I'm a target he ain't likely to miss, even with his eyes closed.'

'Walk with me to the jail,' Hart said. 'I want to talk to you.'

Grat Kane shook his head as Hart left the stable. He turned on his men and gave them orders to take care of the bodies, and to remain together around the stable. Hart fell into step beside the big rancher and they walked along the street towards the law office.

'What's on your mind, Ranger?' Kane asked.

'What's back of the trouble between you and HR? I've been told by my headquarters to look into it, and I shall be talking to Henry Reed when I can get around to him.'

'There's always been friction between the two ranches. I don't reckon I can tell you why. It started long ago, and grew worse with the passing years.'

'There's talk of you planning to divert the stream north of HR.'

74

'Yeah. I heard about it.' Kane laughed.

'Is there any truth in it?' Hart persisted.

'That yarn has been going around for years. If I'd planned to do that then it would have been done long before now. I never even said it in the first place. I reckon someone else did, and folks thought it was me.'

'Why would anyone else say that?'

'To cause trouble, what else?'

'Do you think Henry Reed wants trouble between your two outfits?'

'I doubt it. We neither of us has time for that kind of thing.'

Hart fell silent, his thoughts running deep.

'If I talk with Henry Reed and he gives me similar answers, I'll arrange a meeting between the two of you. Straight talking will clear the air. Would you agree to a meeting?'

'Sure, if Reed means it.'

They reached the office and Hart led the way inside. He picked up the cell keys and ushered Grat Kane into the cell block. Wiley sprang up off the bunk at the sight of his father and came to the door of the cell.

'Get me out of here, Pa.' Wiley grasped the bars and rattled the door.

'Hold your horses.' Grat reached between the bars with a massive hand and secured a grip on Wiley's shirt front. He dragged his son up against the bars and thrust his face close to Wiley's battered visage. 'What's this I hear about you insulting a woman? Is that true?'

'I didn't harm her none, Pa. You know I wouldn't do that. I used her to get away from these law men. They was gonna throw me in jail for nothing at all.'

'If you're lying to me, Wiley, I'll whale the tar out'n you when we get home.'

'I ain't lying, Pa. I'll swear it on the Bible.'

Hart moved along to the next cell, where Charlie Shaw was sitting on his bunk.

'When are you gonna turn me loose?' Shaw asked. 'I got to be getting back to HR.'

'Very soon now. I'll want you to show me the way to HR.'

'Sure thing. You ain't gonna let K Bar get away with anything, are you?'

'Nobody is gonna get away with anything.'

'Wiley got more than he bargained for. Who mussed up his ugly face? How'd you manage to get him into a cell?'

'It was tough, but Wiley is realizing that he ain't tougher than the law.'

Seifert came into the cell block. He caught Hart's eye and jerked his head towards the office, then walked out. Hart followed immediately. Seifert paused by his desk.

'A thought struck me as I came out of the stable,' he said. 'Ossie Payne is always muttering threats against the unknown killer of his son. At the inquest it came out that Billy Payne was in the company of two K Bar riders shortly before he died.'

'Were the K Bar riders named?' Hart asked.

'Yeah. One was Blackie Thomas. We never got the name of the second man. I'm wondering if Ossie has started to make good on his threats.'

'And Thomas is one of the two men killed in the stable,' Hart mused. 'I think we'd better have a word with Payne.'

'Let me talk to him. He'll be a bit difficult. I feel sorry for him, but if he is taking the law into his own hands—' Seifert shrugged and lapsed into silence.

'I'll get rid of Kane.' Hart went back into the cell block.

'Are you gonna turn my boy loose until you decide what to do with him?' Grat asked.

Hart shook his head. 'We can't do that. The charges haven't been worked out yet. He'll have to be patient. Maybe the next time he goes off the rails, he'll think twice before going on the rampage. You'll have to leave now. We've got to start an investigation.'

Grat Kane shook his head. Hart suppressed a sigh.

'I can see what's running through your mind,' he said, 'and my advice to you is don't do it or you'll wind up in a cell.'

'You're that tough, huh?' Grat dropped his hand to the butt of his holstered gun, and the next moment he was gaping into the muzzle of Hart's pistol.

'That's my slow draw,' Hart explained in a matter-of-fact tone, sliding the pistol back into its holster. 'When the chips are down, I'm probably twice as fast.'

'I'm leaving,' Grat said. 'Just bear in mind that if you want me to go along with what you're planning then you've got to give a little yourself. Turn Wiley loose and I'll keep him out at the ranch.'

'I'll think about it.' Hart ushered the big rancher into the front office.

'Are you gonna try and find out who killed Sarn and Thomas?'

'We're working on it. The sooner you leave, the sooner we can get down to it.' Hart crossed to the street door and opened it. 'Go back to your ranch and keep your men out of town until we've done our job. I'll come out to K Bar later.'

Kane opened his mouth to argue, noted the expression in Hart's eyes, and then nodded reluctantly.

'OK. You'll get your chance. I'll expect you at K Bar in about three days. If you don't show up I'll be coming back to town to spring Wiley out of jail, and there won't be much of this place left by the time we get through.'

'Threats are a waste of time,' Hart said easily.

Kane glowered as he mulled over the Ranger's words, and then departed. Seifert came to the door and watched the big rancher stomping along the sidewalk.

'I don't know what promises you've made to Grat, but I sure hope you can keep them,' he said.

'Let's go talk to Payne,' Hart suggested.

They left the office and walked along to the store. Ossie Payne was serving a customer when they entered, and they stood in the background until he was free. Hart studied the storekeeper. Payne was tall and thin, his lean face set in a mask of grief. His dark eyes were narrowed and cold.

'What can I do for you?' he asked, sounding as if each word he spoke was burning his lips.

'We're carrying out a check on all the rifles in town, Ossie.' Seifert kept his tone light and friendly.

'What the hell! And you made me your top suspect, huh?'

'Suspect for what?' Seifert asked.

'I know Luke Warner was shot in the back with a rifle. Because my boy was murdered by K Bar, you suspect me of going out for revenge. I've thought of it, by God, but I've kept my hands clean of murder.'

'All we want to do is check out your rifle, Ossie.' Seifert smiled easily. 'Don't give me a lot of guff. Just get your rifle and we'll check it out. And make it quick, will you? We've got a lot to get through today.'

'Where were you at about this time yesterday?' Hart asked.

'Right here, where I am every day.' Payne studied Hart with an unblinking gaze. 'Who do you suppose would open up the store if I took a day off?'

'Have you left the place at all this morning?' Hart persisted.

'No, I ain't.' Payne reached under the counter and produced a Winchester, which he held out.

'Is it loaded?' Seifert asked as he took the weapon and began to examine it.

'Wouldn't be much use if it wasn't, huh?' Payne thrust out his chin belligerently.

Seifert worked the mechanism of the rifle and a cartridge flew out of the breech. Hart caught it with a deft movement of his left hand and looked it over. There were no scratches on it. Hart shook his head in response to Seifert's unasked question and the deputy walked to the door and fired a shot in the air. Payne flinched at the echoing crash of the rifle. Seifert bent and picked up the spent shell.

'The firing-pin struck dead centre,' he said. 'You got any more long guns around, Ossie?'

'About a dozen. They're all brand new. Do you wanta try them?'

'Not right now,' Hart smiled. 'We'll come back later and talk with you.'

'I ain't going anywhere,' Payne replied. 'You're barking up the wrong tree if you're suspecting me.'

Seifert handed the rifle back to Payne and walked out to the street with Hart following closely. They walked back towards the law office.

'That doesn't prove anything,' Seifert mused. 'Ossie could have several guns stashed away somewhere and we'd never find them.'

'I want to ride out to HR now,' Hart said. 'Turn Shaw loose and he can show me the way.'

'Looks like Ginny has come to enquire when I'm gonna turn Shaw loose,' Seifert observed.

Hart glanced along the sidewalk and saw the girl standing in front of the law office. She was waiting patiently, and a faint smile touched her lips when she saw them advancing towards her.

'Sorry to keep you waiting, Ginny,' Seifert said. 'We've got a lot going against us at the moment. You want to see Charlie, I suppose.'

'I'm tempted to ask Dad to fire him for causing trouble,' she responded. 'I told him yesterday not to take up the problem I had with Pete Downey, and he went against my wishes. We have enough trouble without our men causing more.'

'We haven't seen the worst of it yet,' Seifert said. 'That's why I'm glad Mike is sticking around.'

She turned to Hart, her smile widening. He touched the brim of his hat, smiling in return.

'I hope you're none the worse for that business with Wiley Kane last night,' he said.

'It would have been a whole lot worse if you hadn't been on hand to save me,' she replied. 'I'll never be able to thank you enough.'

'It's all part of the job, miss.' Hart hastened to make light of the incident. 'I don't think Wiley meant to harm you. We're releasing Charlie Shaw now, and I'm gonna ride out to HR with him. I need to talk to your father urgently, and if I'm with Charlie he won't go off on another escapade.'

'I wish you could make him see sense.' Ginny sighed heavily. 'I just don't know where this business is going to end.'

'The trick is not to worry about it.' Seifert unlocked the door of the office. 'Come on in and I'll turn Charlie loose. When you get him back on HR keep him there for a spell. We're trying to get to grips with the trouble and we don't need half-baked idiots like Charlie making it worse.'

Hart followed the girl into the office and she sat down on the chair beside the desk. Seifert took the keys and disappeared through the doorway into the cells. A few moments later, Charlie Shaw emerged from the cells. He grinned sheepishly when he saw Ginny.

'Don't say a word, Charlie,' she said harshly. 'I don't want to hear your excuses. We're riding back to HR now, and you can start thinking up what you'll say to my father when you face him.'

Shaw shrugged. Seifert appeared and handed over Shaw's belongings. He fetched Shaw's gun belt and pistol, and Hart watched the youngster buckle the belt around his waist. Shaw drew the pistol and examined it, and his features hardened as he returned the weapon to its holster.

'I won't go looking for trouble,' Charlie said softly. 'But if that polecat Downey asks for it then he'll get it right in the neck.'

'Get out of here,' Seifert said. 'We don't need you making ripples on the creek. We got enough to settle now.'

'I'm riding to HR,' Hart said, 'and I hope Miss Reed won't mind my company.'

'I shall be glad of it,' she replied with a smile. 'Charlie is in the dog-house right now so your company will be much appreciated, Mr Hart.'

They left the office and walked along the sidewalk to the livery barn. Hart walked with Ginny Reed at his side and Charlie Shaw followed a few paces to their rear. They had passed the saloon when the batwings were thrust open and a harsh voice called out.

'I hear you've been looking for me, Shaw. It's a pity you didn't find me last night. But now is a good time to make your play so turn around and get your gun working.'

Hart whirled, reaching out to push Ginny to one side. He stepped forward two quick paces and reached Shaw's side as the youngster turned to face the speaker.

'Pete Downey, you yellow rat!' Shaw exclaimed. 'Where were you hiding yourself last night?'

Downey was short and thickset, and he was unsteady on his feet. His face was pale, his eyes bleary. Hart dropped his left hand on to Shaw's holster as the youngster readied himself to fight.

'Hold it,' Hart rapped. 'You're drunk, Downey. You'd better go sleep it off. Charlie ain't going to fight, and neither are you.'

'Who in hell are you, sticking your horn in where it ain't wanted? Butt out, mister.'

'I'm a Texas Ranger. Do like I say or I'll jail you.'

'The hell you say! Step aside and keep out of this. It's between Shaw and me. I'm gonna gut-shoot that lily-livered son of a bitch.' Downey dropped his hand to his holstered gun and grasped the butt. 'There ain't no one gonna hunt me around town like I was a dog. You been asking for it a long time, Shaw. Get out from that Ranger and turn her loose.'

Hart stepped in front of Shaw and walked towards Downey, his patience at an end. It was time for a showdown.

SIX

'Back off,' Downey warned. 'You're asking for it, Ranger. I got a score to settle with Shaw, and I'll go through you to get at him.'

Hart halted and drew his pistol. Downey started to draw his gun, but paused when he found himself looking into Hart's muzzle. He lifted his hand away from his pistol, shaking his head.

'So you're the fastest draw I've seen,' he said. 'I guess I made a mistake, huh?'

Hart reached out and relieved Downey of his gun.

'That's better,' he commented. 'Now turn around and head for the law office. You'll be better sleeping it off in a cell. That's the safest place in town right now.'

Downey turned obediently. Hart glanced over his shoulder at Shaw. Ginny was standing motionless on the sidewalk, her face pale and strained.

'This won't take a moment.' Hart smiled. 'I'll meet up with you at the barn.'

Shaw nodded. He was pale, his eyes filled with shock. Hart turned away and escorted Downey to the law office. Seifert took over, and Hart went on to the stable. Shaw was saddling two horses, and Hart prepared his own mount for travel.

They set out back along the street and rode north, taking the trail leading to HR. Hart rode beside the girl, and was anxious to talk to her about conditions on the range, but she seemed remote now, and he could see worry in her eyes. The incident with Downey had distressed her.

Shaw rode ahead, leaving Hart to accompany Ginny. They were some three miles from town when a rifle fired at them from a rise to their left. Shaw fell out of his saddle and lay motionless on the ground. Hart drew his rifle from its scabbard and fired three shots rapidly at the puff of gun smoke marking the ambush position, bracketing the spot. No more shots were fired, and Hart sat for some moments, watching the rise.

'Take a look at Shaw,' Hart said without taking his eyes from the rise.

Ginny obeyed, and called to Hart after a few moments.

'Charlie is hurt bad. He's been hit in the chest.'

Hart decided that the unknown gunman had departed. He rode to where Shaw was lying and stepped down from his saddle, handing his rifle to Ginny as he did so.

'I guess you can use this,' he said.

She nodded and faced the rise, placing the long gun across her saddle and using the horse as cover. She waited, ready for action. Hart bent over Shaw. The youngster was unconscious. There was a patch of blood on his shirt at the left side of his chest. At that moment Hart caught the sound of approaching hoofs and got to his feet, hand easing towards the butt of his pistol. Two riders were coming along the trail from the direction of HR.

'It's my father and Flash Johnson,' Ginny said in a relieved tone.

The two riders came up and dismounted. Johnson bent over Shaw.

'We heard the shots from way back,' said Henry Reed. 'Are you all right, Ginny?'

The girl nodded. She seemed beyond words at that moment.

'Take over here,' Hart said. 'One of you better stay here with Shaw while the other rides into town for a buckboard and the doctor. I think Shaw will be all right, but he's gonna be out of action for some time. I was coming out to HR to talk to you, Reed, but that will have to wait now. I'm going to track down the ambusher.'

'Let Flash side you,' Reed said.

'I ride alone,' Hart responded, shaking his head.

He took his rifle from the girl and swung into his saddle, turning his horse to ride towards the rise.

'I'll catch up with you later,' he said in parting and cantered away, turning in his saddle as he did so to add: 'We need to talk urgently, Reed.'

The rancher nodded and lifted a hand. Hart faced his front and concentrated on the job in hand. He approached the rise cautiously, although he was aware that the ambusher was long gone. When he topped the rise, he saw a line of tracks leading away into the west. He dismounted and walked to the spot where a man had lain in cover, spotted an empty 44.40 shell that was glinting in the grass, and picked it up. Examining the cartridge case, he found it had a long scratch on its side, and the cap had been struck off-centre by the firing-pin.

Hart walked to where the ambusher's horse had been grazing when the shot was fired, and was not surprised, when he examined a cluster of hoofprints, to find that they matched the prints left at the scene of Luke Warner's murder by the killer's horse. He looked around with far-seeing eyes, picking out the direction the ambusher had taken after shooting Shaw, but at that moment he was more interested in the direction from which the ambusher had come. Had the man followed them from Mesquite or chanced on them by coincidence?

If the ambusher had come from the town, was he a townsman? Was he Ossie Payne? Hart checked the ambusher's approach to the spot, and became certain that the man had followed them from town before forging ahead of them to pick his spot to open fire. He remounted and set out trailing the ambusher, certain that he was following the killer of Luke Warner and the two K Bar men back in town.

The morning passed quickly. Hart rode with his Winchester across his saddle, expecting his quarry to turn and fight to maintain his anonymity. The sun blazed down from a cloudless blue sky and heat packed the air, so hot that Hart felt as if he were riding inside a gigantic oven. The tracks led on, showing by their depth that the ambusher was travelling fast and not sparing his horse.

It was around the middle of the afternoon when Hart came upon a shack built beside a narrow stream. He reined in and looked the place over. The prints he was following headed straight towards the little building, but there was no sign of a horse in the immediate area. The place looked derelict. There was a hole in the sod roof and the rawhide door was hanging loose on one hinge.

Hart rode in cautiously, one eye on the tracks he was following, which had stopped in front of the door although the rider had not dismounted. The tracks moved away to the right and kept going. Hart reined in.

'Hello,' he called. 'Anyone home?'

There was no reply. A dense silence held sway around the building. Hart touched spurs to his mount, and was about to pass around the front right-hand corner of the shack when he caught a flicker of movement from the left. The figure of a man had eased forward slightly from the opposite front corner, and sunlight was glinting on the barrel of a pistol in his hand.

Hart hurled himself to his right, kicking his feet clear of the stirrups as he did so. A gun blasted as he vacated the saddle and a bullet zipped by his head as a string of harsh echoes fled across the silent range. Hart hit the ground on his right shoulder. He rolled to the right, and had his pistol in his hand when he regained his feet in a lithe movement.

The man was in the act of levelling his gun for a second shot. Hart fired instinctively. The man jerked backwards out of sight behind the corner, but dropped his pistol, which lay on the ground within Hart's sight. Hart ran to the corner and peered around it, gun ready. The man was down on one knee, gripping his right wrist, and blood showed between his fingers. He gazed up at Hart, shock showing plainly on his weathered features.

'Who are you?' Hart demanded.

'Sam Wishart. I ride for Rafter D.'

'That's Al Denton's place, huh?'

'Yeah. This is his line shack. Who in hell are you?'

'Texas Ranger. Why did you shoot at me?'

'I thought you were up to no good. We've been told to watch for troublemakers. You came sneaking in, looking primed for trouble.'

'I'm tracking a man who ambushed and shot Charlie Shaw. Who's ridden by here in the last two hours?'

'I ain't seen a soul in two days, let alone two hours.'

'You're lying. The tracks I'm following stopped right outside your door, and they ain't two hours old.'

'I ain't seen anyone. I've been out riding the fence. I just got back.'

'Where's your horse?'

'In the corral out back.'

'Get up and let me take a look at you.'

Wishart got to his feet. Hart holstered his gun. He grasped the man's right arm and examined the wrist, which had a long gouge across it.

'You're lucky,' Hart said. 'It ain't serious, but you'd better ride into town and let the doctor look at it.

89

How do I get to Rafter D from here?'

'There's a trail over there which leads to it. The ranch house is about eight miles due west.'

'Get out of here now, Wishart. Saddle and ride.'

Wishart bent to pick up his pistol and Hart kicked it away.

'Leave that. Just get out of here.'

Wishart turned and walked around the shack. Hart followed closely. A horse was standing in a small corral, saddled and bridled. Wishart prepared to travel and then swung into the saddle. He rode out without another glance at Hart, heading in the direction of town.

Hart waited until Wishart had gone. He looked in the shack, which was deserted and unused, then checked out the tracks he was following. They led around the shack and continued into the north-west. Hart went to the corral, checked the tracks made by Wishart's horse, and followed them around the corral. He found the prints coming in along the wire fence that formed the boundary between HR and Rafter D.

So Wishart had been telling the truth. Hart swung into his saddle and continued following the ambusher's tracks. The afternoon was turning into evening, with the sun well over in the western half of the sky. Hart continued relentlessly, ready to follow the tracks into Hell itself.

He mused upon the situation, unable yet to get a picture in his mind of what was happening. There was animosity between HR and K Bar, to the extent that gunplay was erupting between the two ranches.

A killer had struck three times in the past twenty-four hours, slaying K Bar riders. Charlie Shaw, an HR rider, had been shot in an ambush that had been intended to kill him, judging by the strike of the bullet. Grat and Wiley Kane had a reputation for making trouble and, although Grat talked peace and appeared inclined to desire it, Wiley was only half-civilized, and seemed to think he could flout the law and mete out his own brand of justice to anyone who crossed his path. The situation seemed ripe for an explosion, and Hart was aware that he had to act quickly to avert it. He had a niggling thought that a third party was involved somewhere, fanning the flames from time to time.

Just before nightfall, Hart came upon a stretch of rock where the tracks he was following petered out. He cast around in the uncertain light, and was still searching when full darkness came. Halting to make camp, his patience stretched to the limit, he was experienced enough to know that patience was a virtue in his job, but he had walked into this assignment hard on the heels of finishing the previous one and had not found the time to switch mentally. Unwilling to reveal his position by lighting a fire, he ate cold food and drank water from his canteen before turning in, and then slept until the sun came up.

He felt gaunt and hollow when he arose and looked around. The sun was barely above the horizon and he was in the middle of a brooding wilderness. He lit a fire, made a cup of coffee, and fried bacon and beans. The food did much to restore his normally optimistic attitude, and when he was ready to travel he swung into his saddle and took stock of the situation.

The tracks he had been following the previous day had made an unerring line across country, indicating that the rider was heading for a definite destination. The area of rock that had swallowed up the tracks seemed to stretch for miles. Hart got to grips with the problem. He rode back to the spot where the hard ground began and studied the last of the tracks. Looking ahead, he gazed in the direction in which his quarry had been riding, and noted rising ground far ahead. He picked out a spot that seemed to follow the line of tracks and rode towards it.

Nearly two miles later, the rocky ground ended as abruptly as is had begun, and Hart cast around for signs of the hoofprints. It took him an hour to find them going towards the north-east, and he resumed the trail with great satisfaction. The tracks looked as if they had been made hours before, so the rider had not halted during the night and was now miles ahead. Hart took a fresh grip on his patience and continued stoically.

Just before noon he topped a rise and reined in to look at a ranch headquarters which was spread out before him in a low valley. Sunlight glittered on a wide stream that meandered through the low ground. There were several buildings in the yard, most of them clustered together to the left – barns, shacks, and some miscellaneous erections, with three corrals set a little apart. To the right the ranch house stood alone on a knoll; the raised location affording distant views of the vast country.

There was some activity around the yard. A wrangler was busy raising dust in one of the corrals as he pursued his arduous chore of breaking in a horse. Hart heard the sudden beat of hoofs and looked round to see a rider heading towards him. He recognised Ginny Reed, and a sigh escaped him as she reined up at his side.

'Hi, she greeted. 'How did you get on yesterday? Did you catch up with that ambusher?'

'I'm still following him.' Hart indicated the tracks, and explained his actions. 'So here I am, apparently wasting time, and the ambusher has led me to HR, huh?'

'This is our ranch.' She spoke with pride. Dressed in well-cut range clothes, she looked very attractive, and Hart felt his interest quicken as he gazed at her. She looked down at the faint tracks in the dust, a frown creasing her smooth forehead, and when she looked up to meet his gaze her eyes showed puzzlement. 'The ambusher shot Charlie Shaw and has headed here, right into our yard?' she queried.

'That's what it looks like.' Hart gigged his mount forward. 'I'll be interested to find the horse that left these tracks. What happened yesterday after I left you?'

'Dad and Flash took Charlie into town. Doc Wesley says Charlie will be all right in a couple of weeks. We came back to the ranch then.'

'Did you have any trouble out here during the night?' Hart kept his gaze on the tracks, which seemed to be leading straight into the yard of the ranch.

Ginny shook her head. 'There was nothing at all. But I wouldn't expect one man to ride in here and cause trouble. We've got about twenty riders on our payroll and they're primed for anything.'

They reached the stream and Hart saw where the tracks stopped under a cottonwood. He warned Ginny to stay back and dismounted to check around on foot while she sat her mount in the background, watching him intently. Hart walked around the area, studying the ground, and was shaking his head when he eventually returned his attention to the girl.

'The ambusher sat here under the cottonwood and someone came out from the ranch to meet him. It looks like they spent a long time together because there are several cigarette butts on the ground. Then the ambusher rode off in that direction and the man from the ranch went back there.'

'You can tell all that just by looking at the ground?' Ginny demanded.

Hart nodded while his gaze was upon the ranch.

'I don't reckon to be able to find out who came out here last night, but it looks like the ambusher has got a friend on your payroll, and that ain't good because the ambusher must be against HR.'

'Then we've got to find out who met him out here in the night.'

'An easier way will be for me to keep on with these tracks until I come up with the horse that made them,' Hart said. 'But I need to talk to your father before I go any further.' He turned and gazed at the tracks leading away from the ranch. 'What lies in the direction they're heading now?' he asked.

'Rafter D.'

'Uhuh. What kind of a man is Al Denton?'

'Hard-working, and honest, I think.' Ginny nodded as Hart returned to his horse. 'I like Denton. We need more of his sort around here.'

'That's the impression I got when I met him.' Hart touched spurs to his mount, started across the stream, and Ginnie went with him. They cantered towards the ranch. Hart looked around with interest as they entered the yard. 'Nice place you got here,' he observed. 'Have you had any trouble to speak of over the past month?'

'No actual trouble until a couple of days ago. Generally, there's been nothing but tension because of the Kanes. I've always had trouble with Wiley but I can handle him – that is, I could until he grabbed me in the law office. That was a shock because he was always respectful, although he made a nuisance of himself at times.'

'And this business between your father and Grat Kane? There's been a threat to stop the water crossing your range, huh?'

'I don't think Grat Kane ever made that threat, and neither does my father.'

Hart lapsed into silence as they reached the front of the house. They dismounted and looped their reins over the hitching-rail.

'Come into the house and I'll call my father,' Ginnie said.

Hart followed her into the ranch house and looked around appreciatively. The big, square room in which he stood looked as large as a dance-hall, and was well furnished. A large table occupied the centre of the room with ten straight-back chairs ranged around it. A big chandelier was suspended directly above the table and there were numerous lamps on the surrounding walls to complement its light. Thick carpets covered most of the floor-spaces. There were pictures on the walls, and trophies acquired from years of Western living. Several bookshelves lined one wall, and a gunrack occupied pride of place on the wall at the foot of the big staircase that led up to the bedrooms.

'Help yourself to a drink.' Ginny indicated a tray on a sideboard. 'I'll get some cold root-beer after I've called Dad.'

She went to a door in the back wall, opened it and called for her father, and then departed. Hart could hear her voice echoing through the lower rooms of the house. A moment later a male voice answered and footsteps echoed in the passage outside. Henry Reed came into the room, a smile of welcome on his weathered face.

'Glad to see you again, Hart,' he greeted. 'Did you have any luck with that ambusher?'

Hart explained and saw Reed's face turn grim.

'That is bad. It sounds like one of my men is a renegade. That ambusher sure ain't on my side. What do you reckon they were talking about in the dead of night?'

'I might learn the answer to that when I catch up with the ambusher.'

'Do you expect to catch up with him?'

'If his horse doesn't suddenly sprout wings and fly

then I'll follow his tracks until I do get him. I need to ask you what your dealings with Grat Kane are like. What's the word on that threat he was supposed to have made about cutting the water supply to your range?'

'I don't think Kane said such a thing.' Reed shook his head emphatically. 'That rumour has been going the rounds for a couple of years now, and I've heard it a number of times. Personally, I don't have anything to do with the Kanes, but there's never been the hint of trouble from them – until the events of the past couple of days. Now Luke Warner, the K Bar ramrod, has been killed, and two K Bar hands were killed in the stable in town. Then someone put a slug in Charlie Shaw. On the face of it, trouble looks like it has broken out between K Bar and us. But no one on my payroll has lifted a hand against the Kanes. I'd stake my life on that.'

'Unless the man who met the ambusher at the stream in the middle of the night had something to do with it,' Hart observed.

'There's nothing I can do about him until I know who he is. The only way you'll get to him is by taking Charlie's ambusher and making him tell you who his friend is.'

'I want to ask you one question before I move on to do just that. I spoke with Grat Kane in town and sounded him out about meeting you face to face to clear the air. He said OK to that. Would you be agreeable?'

'Sure thing, and the sooner we meet the better, in the light of what is going on now. If Kane's crew ain't causing the trouble, and my men ain't, then who is doing it?'

'That's what I mean to find out.' Hart turned to the door. 'And the sooner I get some answers to the questions bothering me the sooner we'll put a stop to the trouble.' He paused and gazed into Reed's face. 'Has anything happened around here that you can pin on someone?' he asked.

Henry Reed shook his head. 'That's just it. Nothing has gone wrong. I don't understand it.'

'I'll hit the trail then. See you around. I'll let you know about that meeting with Kane when I can set it up.'

Hart left the house and swung into his saddle. He rode steadily back across the valley to where his quarry had waited under the cottonwood. Picking up the trail, he went on, following the faint tracks that formed his only lead to the troublemaker upon whose unknown shoulders the whole situation rested.

SEVEN

Hart halted at noon to rest his horse and eat cold food. He began to relax from the high pinnacle of alertness when he suddenly became aware that his sixth sense had been trying to warn him that he was being followed. His concentration had held the feeling in abeyance until he halted, but there was no mistaking the prickling sensation apparent now between his shoulder-blades. Someone was on his back trail, and had been for some time.

He checked his pistol and long gun before going on, intent upon the seemingly endless trail he was following, but, when he dropped below the skyline of a rise, he dismounted, left his horse standing with trailing reins, and crawled back up the slope. Removing his hat, he raised up cautiously to observe the ground already covered.

Heat haze obscured his vision and he waited patiently for his stalker to come into view. Long minutes passed and the emptiness of the vast range remained undisturbed. He wondered if he were mistaken, but had depended too long upon his senses to disregard any warning they might give him.

Someone was on his back trail, playing a grim game very cautiously.

Hart eventually gave up and returned to his horse, sensing that his stalker was either waiting back there or moving around on one of the flanks to check whether it was safe to continue. Wanting to get his quarry before nightfall, Hart gave in to the urgency of the situation and went on, keeping a watchful eye on his rear as he progressed. He was perturbed by the fact that his senses still warned of someone behind him although he saw nothing untoward.

The tracks had veered from their original direction since leaving HR and had been heading southwest for several hours. The rider seemed to be in no real hurry after leaving the stream at HR, and Hart wondered if the unknown quarry suspected that he was being followed. The tracks were so clear that Hart pushed on faster, his keen nerves balanced on a knife edge of anticipation as he covered the undulating ground. Late evening found him gazing into gathering twilight with the prospect of another night to be spent on the tawny range, which was enveloped in an intense silence that seemed to wrap itself around horse and rider, encompassing them in a trancelike state.

The sky was turning slowly to molten copper beyond the far peaks when Hart noticed a change in the nature of the ground. As the shadows increased around him he saw that the undulating range of short grass was giving way to rolling slopes and cutbanks, and there was just enough light for him to see the tracks he was following turn sharply and enter a dry wash that scarred a long slope. As full dark came he spotted yellow lamplight in the far distance, winking like a beacon, and wondered if his quarry had reached home at last.

Hart sighed as he made camp just short of the wash into which the tracks had led. He wanted to push on but his horse had carried him many miles that day and, although willing to run until it dropped, Hart had to consider the near future. He needed to conserve the strength of the animal in case of emergency.

He made camp, took care of his horse with a drink of water poured into his hat and some oats from the bag he packed behind his cantle, and then sat down to eat his usual cold fare. He was swigging from his canteen when he became aware that someone was approaching furtively.

Hart drew his Colt and cocked it, eyes narrowed as he tried to penetrate the darkness. Stars were glimmering overhead and the horizon to the east carried a faint yellow glow where the moon was rising, and it was enough to enable him to watch his surroundings.

'I got you covered,' he called. 'Declare yourself.'

'It's Ginny Reed and Buck Dolan,' a voice replied without hesitation.

'What in Sam Hill are you doing out here?' Hart was completely surprised. He holstered his pistol and got to his feet as two figures materialized out of the shadows.

'I was worried about you riding into trouble, following those prints.' Ginny's small figure paused before him. Her face was just a pale oval in the night.

'I had a feeling a long way back that I was being followed,' Hart said.

'We stayed behind you in case you found trouble and couldn't handle it.'

'That was a dangerous thing to do.' Hart shook his head. 'Perhaps you'll turn right round and head back to your spread, but, before you go, tell me about the lights I can see from the ridge up there.'

'You're about two miles from Rafter D,' Ginnie said.

'Al Denton's place, huh? I'll be interested to ride into his yard tomorrow, if the tracks head in there.'

'And if they don't?'

'I'll ride on, following those tracks until I do find the horse that made them.'

'You're not pleased to see me out here, are you,' Ginnie demanded.

'No. I appreciate your concern, but what would I say to your father if something bad happened to you?'

'I'm pretty safe with Buck. He won't let anything happen to me. We'll turn round and head back to the ranch now. I hope you'll get your man, Ranger.'

'I'll be back to your place after I've run him to earth,' Hart said.

The girl and her escort faded back into the shadows and, a moment later, Hart heard the sounds of two horses departing. He listened intently until full silence returned, then shook his head and turned into his blankets to sleep.

The sun was just below the eastern horizon when Hart broke camp next morning, and full daylight arrived as he rode out. He checked the hoofprints he had been following, and entered the wash to continue, emerging lower down with a clear view of Al Denton's Rafter D before him. He saw at a glance that the hoofprints went straight on towards the ranch.

The cow spread was a hive of activity when he reached it. Several men were in the process of moving out, and there were more just clear of the ranch, heading away to the east. Hart saw where riders had come out of the yard and gathered around the prints he had been following before going on, inadvertently obliterating the trail. He spotted Al Denton standing on the porch of the ranch house, and noted that the man had a rough sling supporting his left arm.

Hart rode up to the porch and halted. Denton looked shocked. His face was pale, his eyes narrowed.

'Howdy, Ranger,' he greeted. 'You've sure turned up at the right moment. We've been shot at by some galoot who came out of the dawn and hammered the place with rifle fire. Two of my men are dead and three wounded, including me. My crew picked up tracks out there and are out hunting the ambusher. How'd you come to be riding in from the direction the man used?'

'I've been following that ambusher's tracks for the best part of a day.' Hart shook his head. 'He sure gets around.' He explained his movements and the events that had triggered them. 'This turn of action was the last thing I expected,' he mused. 'I had hoped I'd run my man to earth here, and I sure wish your men had stayed clear of his tracks.'

'I'll send a rider to stop them.' Denton waved to one of the riders patrolling the yard. 'Why don't you get down and settle until I get word back from the trackers? I sure wish you had showed up an hour ago. It would have saved Jake and Pete. Trouble is breaking out all over the county since Luke Warner was killed. Do you think Grat Kane is on the warpath because his foreman was shot dead?'

'I got no opinion about that. My job is to learn facts and act on my findings. You probably don't know it, but two more K Bar riders were gunned down in town yesterday morning.'

'The hell you say!' Denton grasped his left elbow, grimacing as pain struck through the limb. 'Did you get that outlaw you were chasing?'

'Yeah. He's behind bars right now.'

'Did he shoot Luke Warner?'

'I'm satisfied he didn't.' Hart stepped down from his saddle and stretched as a rider came up. He listened to Denton's instructions for the men on the trail of hoofprints.

The rider departed at a gallop and Denton motioned for Hart to join him on the porch.

Is there anything you need?' the rancher asked. 'Have you eaten this morning?'

'I've been on cold food since yesterday.' Hart grimaced.

'Walk over to the cook-shack. Breakfast is hardly over. It was rudely interrupted this morning. If you need any supplies then tell the cook and he'll give you whatever you're short on. I'll be riding into town this morning. It's about time the local law got their teeth into this situation. I hope you get your man. I'll be mighty interested in who the hell it was coming in here and shooting up the place. To my way of thinking, it can only be the Kanes at the back of it.'

'Thanks. I'll keep you informed of my progress.'

Hart led his horse across to the cook-shack. He was given an ample breakfast and two cups of good, strong coffee by the nervous cook, who was generous with his supplies, and when Hart rode out his gunnysack containing his store of supplies was bulging. He left the ranch and followed the tracks of the riders who had been tailing his quarry, and came up with them as they were returning to the Rafter D.

'When you catch that sonofabitch, bring him back to Rafter D and we'll string him up,' one of the cowboys said heatedly.

'The law will string him up after his trial,' Hart responded, and rode on.

The tracks had turned south, and Hart checked them carefully before riding on. He now had a rough idea of the lay-out of the area, and sensed that he was riding towards K Bar. He kept an open mind as he followed the interminable tracks, and was wary of the inevitable ambush that would result if his quarry turned at bay.

An hour later he heard shooting in the distance and touched spurs to his horse. He kept an eye on the tracks, which were heading in the same direction, and, topping a ridge, he pulled his horse into a dust-raising halt. A stagecoach was halted just ahead – one of its six horses down in the dust. A robbery was evidently in progress. The lone robber was on top of the coach, busy rifling through the contents of the baggage piled there.

Hart saw three figures lying on the ground beside the coach. He spurred his horse and went forward at a gallop. The robber's horse was standing with trailing reins at the rear of the coach. Hart drew his pistol. The robber caught the sound of his approach and looked up. Hart fired a warning shot over the man's head.

The man drew his gun and prepared to fight. Hart snapped another shot instantly, and saw the robber jerk before twisting and falling off the side of the coach. The figure hit the ground, tried to get up, and then fell on his face. Gun echoes were fading into the distance as Hart reined in at the grim scene. The robber was plainly dead. The single shot had taken him through the centre of the chest. One of the three figures beside the coach was moving slightly, and Hart dismounted quickly.

'Take it easy,' he said, seeing that the man was wounded in the chest.

'Did you nail that robber?' the man demanded weakly. 'I'm the coach-driver. We saw a rider coming towards us, and he pulled a gun just before we reached him. He shot my guard without warning and then plugged me.'

'He's dead,' Hart said. He checked the man's wound, stanched the bleeding and then examined the other two men. Both were dead. He went around the coach to where the robber was lying and looked him over intently. The man was a stranger, aged about thirty-five, and had the look of a long rider about him. Hart wasted little time on him. It would be up to others to try and identify him.

He spent more time on the horse the man had ridden. Checking the animal's hoofs, he verified that the tracks he had followed for almost a day had been made by the same animal as had carried the killer of Luke Warner from the stream where the ambush had taken place.

Hart drew the rifle out of the scabbard on the horse and fired a shot in the air. When he checked the cartridge case that was ejected he found the tell-tale scratch on it and also the off-centre mark made by the firing-pin on the cap. He gazed down at the features of the unknown dead man, and was disappointed that the death of the robber neatly closed the door on his only worthwhile line of investigation.

Hart went back to the coach-driver and questioned him. The coach had been on its way to the village of Oak Creek, which was four miles ahead, where it was scheduled to turn north again to Mesquite. Hart loaded the driver and the dead men, including the robber, into the coach, put the robber's horse in harness with the team, and tied his own horse behind. He climbed up to the driving-seat and set the coach into motion.

Oak Creek was a small collection of buildings beside an irregular stretch of water. A blacksmith was hammering metal in a forge. Hart stopped the coach beside it and stepped down into the dust. The smith, a big man with powerful arms, looked up at Hart, then put down his hammer and picked up a twist of rag to wipe sweat from his gleaming torso.

'Is there a doctor around here?' Hart asked. He introduced himself and explained the situation. The smith peered out at the coach.

'There's only Heck Jones,' he said. 'He doctors animals, but he'll help anyone in trouble. I'll fetch him. He'll be in the bar along the street.'

Hart untied his horse from the back of the coach and led the animal to a nearby water-trough. When the horse-doctor arrived – a small man with beady eyes and a wide forehead – they lifted the coach-driver out of the vehicle and carried him into the smith's house.

'He'll live, I reckon,' Jones opined after a quick examination. 'He oughter see a real doctor – Doc Wesley in Mesquite is the nearest. But I reckon the ride there now will do him more harm than good. I'll put him up in my place. Who else is in the coach?'

'They need an undertaker, not a doctor,' Hart said. 'One is the shotgun guard, the second is a passenger, and the third is the robber.'

'Frank Willen was due in on that coach today,' Jones said. 'We better look at faces. It'll be a bad thing if Frank is one of them. He's got a wife and two kids here.'

They went back to the coach and Jones uttered a curse when he looked at the dead men.

'That's Frank Willen all right. And that one is Art Rogers, the shotgun guard. Is that the robber?' He went close and studied the robber's slack features. 'He's a stranger to me. Never seen him before.'

'I'll drive the coach to Mesquite,' Hart said. 'You

better take Willen off here.'

The dead passenger was lifted out of the coach and laid on the ground beside the smithy. Several people were arriving, attracted by the unusual activity around the coach, and Hart made haste to get under way. He retied his horse behind the vehicle and paused beside the smith to ask directions to Mesquite.

'Just follow the track over there.' The man pointed off to the right. 'It'll take you right into Mesquite.'

Hart climbed into the driving-seat and took up the reins. He kicked off the brake, cracked the whip, and sighed in relief as the coach jerked forward and began to roll with grating wheels. Hoofs pounded the sun-baked ground as the horses threw their combined weight against their collars.

The drive to Mesquite was uneventful, and night was falling when Hart reached the main street. Flaring lamps threw yellow patches of light across the dust. Hart reined up in front of the law office and sat for a moment considering the past twenty-four hours. Then he stepped down to the sidewalk and went into the office, where Lew Seifert sat behind the desk, looking as if he had not moved since Hart left him the day before.

The deputy roused himself after Hart had given him a run-down of his activities, and went out to the coach to view the robber. He came back frowning and shaking his head.

'I got a feeling I've seen that robber's face somewhere,' he mused, going to the desk and producing a stack of wanted posters.

'There's no urgency about him now he's dead,' Hart said. 'Tomorrow will do to try and identify him. But he's the man who dry-gulched Luke Warner. The horse he was riding made the prints I followed from the spot where Charlie Shaw was ambushed through to the coach robbery, and the rifle I found in the saddle scabbard on the horse is the one we've been looking for. It makes the scratch on the used shell when it is ejected, and the firing-pin strikes off-centre.'

'That's a helluva note!' Seifert gazed into Hart's eyes. 'That rifle was the one that killed Sarn and Thomas in the stable, and it was used to shoot Charlie Shaw from cover.'

'And the killer rode into Rafter D and threw slugs into the place, killing two of the outfit and wounding three others. To wind up, he robbed the coach and killed the shotgun guard and a passenger, and wounded the driver. He had a pretty busy twenty-four hours that has given us a mighty big problem.'

'The horse and the rifle link the robber to all those killings,' Seifert mused. 'We've got the job of proving he did it.'

'And why!' Hart shook his head. 'I guess we've got to identify him first of all. We know he was in town when Sarn and Blackie were shot, so someone must have seen him. He would have used the saloon, I guess, and probably the store. Get people in to view the body. We've got to trace his movements around here and find who he contacted when he first rode in. It's the only lead we'll get now he's dead.'

Seifert pushed aside the stack of wanted dodgers

110

he had been scanning.

'He's not among them,' he said. 'I'll get on to the job of identifying him and checking his movements.'

'What's been happening around here since I rode out with Charlie Shaw and Ginny Reed?' Hart asked.

'The place has been as quiet as Boot Hill on a Sunday evening. There ain't been trouble in any shape or form. Looks like you're the only one to have had difficulties. Al Denton rode in around noon today with his arm in a sling and news of his place getting shot up. I've been looking around town, checking rifles with no luck. Grat Kane rode in early this afternoon and tried to get me to turn Wiley loose until a trial is fixed, but he didn't even start shouting when I refused. Usually, Grat is like a mad bull when he can't get his own way.'

'I'm going out again tomorrow to look at the tracks around the stream where Luke Warner was found,' Hart mused. 'Instead of tracking them from there, I want to back-track them to where they came from. I might get some answers that way.'

'Ain't you had enough of them tracks? They would have driven me loco if I'd had to follow them. I'd never want to see another set of tracks for the rest of my life.'

'They're all I've got to work on at the moment. I'll be riding out at first light tomorrow. Take care of that coach and the bodies, huh? I need a drink and some grub. Let's hope it's gonna be a quiet night. I could do with a few hours in a bed.'

'Leave everything to me,' Seifert said. 'I'll put your horse away, too.'

Hart left the office and paused for a moment, looking at the coach, wishing he could have prevented the attempted robbery. He sighed and walked along the street, heading for the saloon, his thirst becoming more apparent with every step he took, and tiredness racked his powerful body.

He sensed that the little town had an atmosphere of stillness about it, and wondered whether it was brooding by the townsmen over violence that was yet to come or whether his own sense of anticipation was supplying the sensation. The saloon was quiet, although nearly a score of men were inside. The murders of the previous day had evidently caused suspicion to take hold, for a muted hubbub of voices and an air of fear was unmistakable. Hart wondered what would happen when the news of the coach robbery and the killings became known.

Hart drank a beer and left almost immediately, declining an invitation to join Doc Wesley at his table, although he checked with the doctor about the condition of Charlie Shaw.

'He'll survive,' Wesley said. 'Have you made any progress with your investigation?'

Hart shook his head, recalling the countless miles he had travelled with only a mystery to show for his efforts. But that was the way with his job. He had to work through the fruitless grind of digging for clues until he made a breakthrough. He left the saloon, went along to the café for a meal, and felt more human by the time he had blunted his pangs of hunger.

Standing in the shadows on the street, feeling

strangely restless and ill at ease, Hart let his mind roam over past events. They seemed to have been random, coincidental, each an isolated happening, but bitter experience had taught him that most bad things occurring during an investigation were but disjointed parts of the whole situation confronting him. It all seemed a mystery because at the moment he did not have enough background knowledge of the coach robber or who was running the local trouble.

He sifted mentally through the facts he did know, looking for links, seeking to connect strands of guilt with those men he had come into contact with during the past day. Wiley Kane was in jail, where he could do nothing to incriminate himself further, and Hart wondered if he could benefit from the big man's release, bearing in mind that some innocent might get killed in the process. Wiley Kane was a violent man who could not conceal his actions under a cloak of innocence. If Wiley was involved in the trouble then he would go ahead regardless of whether he was incriminating himself. It was the only good point Hart could find in the whole tapestry of trouble.

But there was an indication that a third party was involved in the cat-and-mouse game which was being played in the background quite apart from the obvious sides represented by HR and K Bar. Grat Kane seemed to be a contradiction – emanating menace while professing to want peace and accord. Then there was the storekeeper, Ossie Payne, whose son had been murdered. Hart moved restlessly. He had thought that locating the rifle that had been used to shoot Luke Warner and the others would have revealed the whole violent plot, but here he was facing an even deeper mystery.

Hart straightened, thinking it was time to turn in. He wanted to be out and riding before the sun showed next morning, but at that moment he heard drumming hoofs just out of town, approaching rapidly. Coming unexpectedly through the stillness of the night, the sound seemed filled with a grim urgency. He dropped a hand to his gun butt as two riders appeared on his left and raised dust along the centre of the street all the way to the law office.

Hart hurried in the same direction, aware that no one rode at such a breakneck pace through the night unless it was a matter of life and death. The riders dismounted and hastened into the office, and Hart began to run, fearful of the developments that were about to be revealed.

EIGHT

The law office door was half open when Hart reached it, and he stepped aside as a man emerged in a hurry. They almost collided, and Hart grasped the man's arm and held him as he moved away to run along the street.

'What's the trouble?' Hart demanded.

'I need to find the doctor. Henry Reed has been shot. Ginny is in the office telling Seifert about it.'

'Doc Wesley is in the saloon,' Hart told him.

The man set off at a run and Hart entered the office. Ginny Reed was seated on a chair beside the desk with Seifert bending over her. The girl was clearly distressed; speaking rapidly in a high-pitched tone. She got to her feet when she saw Hart, and he could see that she had been crying. Her eyes were over-bright and red-rimmed.

'Sit down, Ginny,' Seifert said consolingly. 'You've done all you can. Doc Wesley is a good man. He'll ride out to HR soon as he gets the word. Just calm down and tell us what happened.'

'Dad was standing on the porch this afternoon,

115

talking to Flash Johnson about taking precautions around the spread. There was the sound of a shot and Dad fell, hit in the chest.' Ginny lifted her gaze to Hart's set features. 'I went out with Buck and we found the spot where the ambusher fired from, although he was long gone by the time we got there. It was by that cottonwood where the man you were trailing earlier met someone from the ranch.'

'I remember the spot,' Hart said. 'Is your father badly hurt, Ginny?'

'I don't think his life is in danger, but he lost a lot of blood. Cookie patched him up, and that should hold him until we get back with the doctor.'

The street door was opened and Buck Dolan entered. He was breathing heavily, his eyes narrowed, filled with a harsh glitter.

'Doc will be riding out in a few minutes,' he reported. 'We'll go back with him, huh, Ginny?'

'You bet!' The girl nodded.

'Did anyone on the ranch get a look at the ambusher?' Hart demanded.

'We reached that cottonwood within five minutes of the shot being fired, but there was no sign of anyone around,' Ginny said. 'I sent a couple of men to follow his tracks, and I hope they've got him by the time we get back to HR.'

'I hope you'll find your father comfortable when you get there,' Hart said. 'I'll be out tomorrow at dawn to check on the ambusher.'

Ginny nodded and got to her feet. She staggered as she walked to the door and Hart half-lifted a hand to steady her as she passed him but desisted at the last moment. She smiled wanly at him and went out to the street. Dolan followed her closely, and a moment later Hart heard the sound of their horses clopping along the street.

'What do you make of that?' Seifert mused. 'It's a helluva note when a man can't stand in his own yard without getting shot. And now we've tied down the question of the rifle used in all the killings, someone else has started ambushing people, and this time Henry Reed has been hit. It's all a big mystery to me. I went round most of the town in the last twenty-four hours, looking for that rifle until I was cross-eyed, and it's no wonder I didn't find the darn thing; it wasn't even here.'

'I don't want to horn in and tell you your job,' Hart said, 'but you've got to find if there is a link between the coach robber and anyone in town. We can't make any more progress until we know what's going on around here.'

'What are you gonna do?' Seifert moved towards the door.

'I'm through for today. I've got another long haul tomorrow. I'll check with you before I pull out in the morning. I need to track down the man who shot Henry Reed. He could lead us to that mysterious third party agitating in the background.'

Hart left the office and paused while Seifert locked the door. They walked along the street together as far as the saloon, and Hart kept going as the deputy turned aside to shoulder through the batwings. Hart entered the hotel and picked up the key to his room, his mind working over the salient

117

points of the trouble, picking at them like a dog worrying a bone. He needed answers, and fast.

He had one foot on the bottom stair when a slight movement off to his left caught his eye. He turned his head quickly, his gun leaping into his hand, and saw Trig Dexter emerging from the dining-room. The gunman half-lifted both his hands, blinking at the speed of Hart's draw.

'Have you got a minute?' the K Bar gunnie asked.

'What's on your mind?' Hart returned the pistol to his holster.

'Grat wants to talk to you. I've been waiting a long time for you to show.'

'Why didn't he come into the law office in the usual way?' Hart thrust out his bottom lip as he considered.

'He doesn't want to be seen. He's waiting in the stable. I can tell you he ain't the type to skulk around, but he ain't gonna set himself up as a target for that killer who nailed our two men yesterday.'

'What does he want? I ain't about to turn Wiley loose, if that's what he's got on his mind.'

'You'll have to talk to him to find out what's on his mind, and I don't have to tell you that what Grat Kane wants, he gets.'

'Not while I'm around,' Hart retorted.

Dexter grinned. Hart shook his head and went out to the street. He paused for Dexter to follow, and was surprised to see the gunman remaining in the hotel.

'You're not coming along?' Hart called.

'I don't agree with everything Grat does, and he can't force me into something I don't want to do.'

'So what's he planning that's against your principles?'

'Go and ask him. I've done my job by telling you he wants to see you. The only thing I want to kill tonight is my thirst.'

Hart went to the stable. A lantern was burning over the open doorway, and he experienced a shiver of anticipation along the length of his spine as he approached. But he did not think Grat Kane would set a gun trap for him right here in town. He entered the stable and paused on the threshold to look around.

Grat Kane was standing in a stall with two hard-faced gunnies flanking him. The big man grunted with satisfaction when he saw Hart, and came lumbering forward, accompanied by his watchful men.

'I want Wiley out of jail right now,' Grat said in his deep, grating voice.

'You're wasting your time.' Hart shook his head. 'Wiley is safely out of the way behind bars. If he was on the loose there's no telling what he might get up to. He might even get himself killed, the way he defies the law. Why don't you leave well alone and be thankful he's where he is? Someone is killing K Bar crew, and Wiley could be on the list.'

'I ain't taking no for an answer. There's a man up in the hayloft with a gun covering your back, and he'll shoot you if I don't get what I want. Ordinarily I wouldn't go against the law, but I'm desperate right now. I heard there's gonna be a raid on the jail by a bunch of men who reckon to lynch Wiley. It's part of the plot to push K Bar into a fight, and I'll kill anyone who tries to put a rope around my boy's neck. Wiley has pulled some bad tricks in his time, but he ain't done a thing he oughter be hanged for.'

'No one is gonna take Wiley out of that jail – not you or a lynch mob.' Hart spoke confidently. 'When is the mob supposed to strike? The town is quiet. There's no one talking about taking the law into their own hands.'

'They'll be riding in around midnight.' Kane lifted a hand impatiently. 'That's enough jawing. Are you gonna turn my boy loose? Any time you want to bring him to trial I'll make sure he turns up to face it.'

'I've got nothing more to say about it. As far as I'm concerned, Wiley stays in jail until his trial.'

Hart gazed into Grat Kane's taut face. There was a glint in the big man's dark eyes as he returned the gaze. Then Grat shook his head and sighed heavily. His prominent belly wobbled as he sucked in a fresh breath, and he waved a ponderous hand.

'You got anything yet on who killed my foreman? Luke was a good man. He didn't deserve to die like that. I'll want to see the man that killed him.'

'I thought you said you knew where to look for his killer.'

'I ain't the man to go off half-cocked. I've got to be sure of myself before I take steps. But we'll have Luke's killer for breakfast, no matter how long it takes.'

Hart was slowly gaining the impression that Kane was stalling for time, keeping him talking here while something was happening elsewhere. He thought of

Wiley in the jail and an alarm bell rang in his mind. He turned swiftly and ran out to the street, ignoring Kane's call to stop. When he saw several horses standing in front of the law office he sprinted in that direction.

He was still fifty yards from the law office when a number of men emerged from it and climbed hurriedly into the saddles of the waiting horses. One of them was an outsize figure, and Hart did not need to be told that it was Wiley Kane. He drew his pistol, and at that moment someone emerged from a doorway to his right and collided with him.

Hart went sprawling off the sidewalk and fell heavily before rolling in the dust of the street; such was the force of the impact. He sprang up instantly, but by the time he had picked up his gun and looked for the departing riders they were mere shadows in the darkness, riding fast out of town. Hart turned to look for the man who had collided with him and found himself alone. He heard the sound of retreating footsteps in an adjacent alley before silence settled.

Shaking his head, Hart went on to the law office. The door stood ajar and he entered with levelled gun, although he was aware that he was wasting his time. The connecting door in the back wall was wide open. He crossed to it, peered into the cell block, and a bitter sigh escaped him when he saw that Wiley was indeed gone, and Gimp Alder had been released.

'What's going on here?'

Hart turned at the sound of the voice and saw Lew Seifert coming into the office. The deputy's expression showed that he feared the worst, and his shoulders slumped when Hart explained the situation. Hart holstered his pistol.

'Let's go and pick up Grat Kane,' he said angrily. 'He kept me talking at the stable while his men busted Wiley out of here.'

'The hell you say! I wouldn't want to try and arrest Grat unless a posse was backing me.' Seifert shook his head.

'I'll handle him myself,' Hart rapped.

He departed quickly and hastened along the street to the stable. He found the place empty and clenched his teeth in frustration. He had been outsmarted, and it hurt. Going back along the sidewalk, he paused at the batwings of the saloon and peered into the long room. Trig Dexter was seated at a small table, and Hart thrust through the swing-doors to stalk across the brightly lit room to Dexter's side.

The gunman looked up at Hart's approach and a thin smile flitted across his lean face. Hart felt his temper rise but took a grip on his emotions.

'I guess you knew what Grat was planning, huh?' he demanded.

Dexter shrugged. 'It's none of my business what my boss gets up to when I ain't around to watch him.'

'You knew he planned to bust Wiley out of jail,' Hart insisted.

'I heard him talking about it but I didn't think he would be stupid enough to go through with it. I advised against it, but Grat is a law unto himself. He doesn't give a damn about consequences. His boy was in jail and Grat wanted him out, so now Wiley is free.'

'Not for long, and when I throw Wiley back behind bars, Grat will be with him. Get on your feet, Dexter. I'm arresting you as an accessory to the jail-break.'

'You won't make that stick.' Dexter froze and his eyes took on a cold expression. 'Don't add to your problems by locking horns with me, Ranger.'

'Get on your feet and put your hands up. I said you're going to jail.'

Dexter sat motionless, and Hart could almost sense the gunman's brain working, weighing up the situation. Then Dexter laughed mirthlessly.

'OK. We'll play it your way. I ain't gonna set myself up against the law because Grat acted like a fool. My turn will come later. This whole deal is gonna explode into real trouble before much longer.'

He stood up and lifted his hands shoulder-high. Hart relieved him of the pistols holstered on his hips and Dexter dropped his hands to his sides as he walked easily to the door. Hart had the feeling that he was doing the wrong thing but he was angry at the way he had been fooled.

They went to the law office. Seifert was outside with the undertaker, who was supervising the removal of the bodies from the coach. About a dozen townsmen were standing in a silent group in front of the office, watching the grim scene. Hart paused as the body of the robber was placed on the sidewalk.

'Take a look at his face, men,' Seifert said, and the spectators edged forward. 'Tell me if you can identify

123

him.' He paused, waiting for a reply, but none came. 'Has anyone seen him around town?' Seifert persisted. 'He's been around for a couple of days. Someone must have seen him.'

There was no reply from the townsmen, and Hart motioned for Dexter to precede him into the office. He locked Dexter in a cell, and returned to the office as Seifert came in from the street.

'So where's Grat?' Seifert asked.

'Long gone by the time I reached the stable,' Hart said through his teeth.

'I expected that.' Seifert shook his head. 'What's Dexter been up to?'

'Nothing I can charge him with. I threw him in a cell to relieve my feelings. Turn him loose in the morning.'

'So what shall we do about Wiley?'

Hart grimaced. 'Thinking about it, I reckon his escape was the best thing that could have happened. Wiley won't let the grass grow under his feet. We won't have to wait long for developments where he is concerned. Perhaps Grat has done us a good turn after all, busting Wiley out. I did tell him that jail was the safest place for Wiley at this time. Let's just hope that no innocent bystander will get hurt if Wiley goes off the rails again.'

'About that dead robber.' Seifert shook his head. 'I can't believe he was around town a couple of days and no one saw him. Do you reckon he was working for someone – that third party who's supposed to be stirring things up between HR and K Bar?'

'We'll never know if we can't get him identified.'

'I'll make everyone in town take a look at him tomorrow,' Seifert said grimly.

'I planned to ride out to HR early, but I'll stick around town to try and get a line on the robber,' Hart decided. 'I guess I can call it a day now, huh?'

Seifert nodded and Hart left the office. He walked along the street to the hotel and entered to go up to his room. His tiredness was overwhelming, and he dropped on to the bed and closed his eyes, not even bothering to remove his gun belt. He was asleep within moments, and lay as dead until the sun came up next morning.

Stirring, Hart stifled a yawn and got to his feet. He found some water in a jug beside a tin basin and washed his face. He was still tired, but moved around with deadly intent. He needed a breakthrough in this situation, and the only way of getting it would be a positive identification of the dead robber. He went down to the hotel dining-room and ate breakfast, then departed for the law office, entering to find Lew Seifert already at his desk.

The deputy threw the bunch of cell-keys across the desk. 'You can have the pleasure of turning Dexter loose,' he said. 'He's been rattling the bars of his door since daybreak. We don't need him, do we?'

'No. If we do want him we can always put our hands on him.' Hart picked up the keys and went into the cell block.

Trig Dexter was pacing his cell like a trapped cougar. He halted when he saw Hart, and a scowl came to his face.

'You're pushing this too far,' he snarled. 'You ain't

125

got any cause to hold me.'

'You want to make something of it?' Hart countered, and Dexter firmed his lips.

'Just turn me loose,' he rasped.

Hart unlocked the cell door and stepped aside. Dexter left the cell and walked with hurried steps into the office, moving fast, as if he could not bear to remain in the jail a moment longer than necessary. Hart followed him, smiling grimly, and watched Seifert hand Dexter his belongings. Dexter checked his pistols and eased them into his holsters.

'Thanks for nothing,' he said tightly, and departed.

Hart glanced at Seifert and grimaced.

'How soon can we get people looking at the robber?' he asked.

'It is kind of important.' Seifert grinned. 'I guess I better do the inviting to view because I know everyone in town. You can stand by the body and get the reactions of the viewers, huh?'

'That sounds like a good way of handling it. Try getting in folk who might have come into contact with the robber – stableman, bartender, and so on. Someone must have seen him around.'

'You go along to the undertaker's place and wait there. Nick Tarleton is a good man. He'll help all he can. His mortuary is on the back lots. You can get to it along the alley this side of the saloon.'

Hart nodded and departed. He looked around the town as he walked along the street. A heavy silence lay across the community. There were few people out at this early hour, and Hart felt a sense of anticipation take hold of him. He needed to do several important things today, but was aware that he had to take them singly, and identifying the dead robber was the most important item on his grim agenda.

He turned into the alley beside the saloon and walked along to the back lots. A house was standing about fifty yards behind the saloon, with a couple of smaller buildings flanking it. A tall, thin man was opening a wide gate in a six-foot fence. He paused and watched Hart's approach.

'You must be the Ranger,' he called. 'I'm Nick Tarleton, the undertaker. I've got that robber all spruced up and ready to be looked at. Have you found out anything about him yet?'

Hart shook his head.

'No, but give folk time to jog their memories. Someone must have seen him around, and we should hear about it soon.'

'I got a piece of evidence out of his shirt-pocket when I stripped him last night.' Tarleton dug into a pocket and produced a small sheet of paper, which he handed to Hart. 'What do you make of that?'

Hart took the paper; a banker's draft for $200, signed by Ossie Payne.

'Knowing Ossie like I do,' Tarleton said, shaking his head, 'I don't believe he would sign a cheque for that kind of money even if he had a gun pointed at his head.'

'Perhaps he was paying for services rendered.' Hart put the draft in his breast pocket. 'I'll have to follow this up now. If anyone turns up to view the body while I'm gone, get their reactions, huh?'

'Sure thing. And watch your step with Ossie. He ain't been his normal self since young Billy was killed.'

'Thanks.' Hart turned away, his thoughts turning rapidly.

Hart traversed the alley beside the store until he reached the main street. The store was open and he entered to find Ossie Payne behind the long counter, filling up shelves with merchandise. Payne looked up quickly at the sound of Hart's boots, and then lunged sideways to reach under the counter. When he straightened, Hart saw a shotgun coming into view.

With no time to think, Hart reached for his pistol, calling a warning as he did so. Payne kept moving, his face showing desperation. Hart could see the long-barrelled weapon swinging up to cover him. He threw his pistol up into the aim and fired swiftly to save his life.

NINE

Hart's gun blasted out the silence, booming in the confined space of the store, making cans rattle on the shelves. In the split second of firing, he lifted his gun muzzle slightly and aimed for a shoulder shot, mindful of the shotgun swinging to cover him. Payne jerked as the .45 slug hit him, and was pushed off aim. His finger tightened convulsively on the trigger of the shotgun and the big weapon thundered, hurling a load of buckshot across the store.

Hart dropped to the floor just before the storm of lead spurted from the muzzle. He arose swiftly; pistol levelled, and saw Payne leaning back against the shelves, the shotgun slipping from his grasp. A patch of blood was spreading rapidly across his right shoulder. Hart grimaced at the stink of burned powder pervading his nostrils and went forward to where Payne was slipping to the floor. He went around the counter and bent over the man. Payne was unconscious, and Hart, needing answers, was relieved to find him still alive.

Hart's ears were ringing with the thunder of the shooting. He straightened, and, turning swiftly as someone came into the store, was relieved to see Seifert standing on the threshold, a gun in his hand.

'What in hell happened?' Seifert could not see Payne lying behind the counter.

Hart explained, and the deputy came forward to look down at the unconscious storekeeper.

'Jeez!' he gasped. 'I'll fetch Doc Wesley.'

He departed. Hart returned to Payne, but there was nothing he could do. His ears were protesting at the noise of the shooting and he forced a yawn to clear them. His mind was niggling over the problems facing him, and in the forefront of his thoughts was the question of Payne's violent reaction to his arrival in the store.

It seemed an age before Seifert returned with Doc Wesley. Hart stepped back while the doctor carried out a cursory examination. Wesley tut-tutted.

'Have him carried over to my place,' he directed briskly. 'He's in a bad way, but I should be able to save him if we act quickly.'

'Try to bring him round,' Hart said. 'We need to talk to him real bad.'

Wesley shook his head, his expression harsh. He hurried out, and Seifert went to the street door, where a group of townsmen was already gathering. Four men came in to bear Payne away. Hart relaxed slightly, heaving a long sigh as he forced himself to alleviate the shock of the grim experience.

'Does Payne have a wife?' he asked.

'Yeah. She went back East to stay with relatives after young Billy was killed. That was six months ago, and it looks like she ain't gonna come back. Show me that banker's draft. You said Ossie reached for his shotgun soon as he saw you. He must have had a guilty conscience. I reckon he heard about the robber being brought in dead and figured you called this morning to arrest him.'

'You're quick on giving him a motive,' Hart mused. 'I'm keeping an open mind until I've heard what Payne has to say about his actions.'

'And if he dies before we can talk to him we'll be in a heap of trouble.' Seifert shook his head. 'You better go along to the doc's and stand by. I'll tell Tarleton to stop the viewing of the body until we've had a talk with Ossie. He might be able to clear up a number of the questions running through my mind.'

Hart nodded and left the store. He drew a deep breath of fresh air as he went along the street, followed by the group of bystanders. Another group was gathering outside the doctor's office, attracted by the four men carrying the inert body of Ossie Payne.

Questions were thrown at Hart as he entered the doctor's office, but he waved them away, shaking his head. A middle-aged woman appeared and introduced herself as Doc Wesley's wife. Hart explained his business and was greeted warmly.

'You'd better come this way,' Ellen Wesley said, opening a door.

Hart entered a big room and found Wesley bending over the inert figure of Ossie Payne, whose shirt had been removed. The doctor was probing for the bullet in Payne's shoulder and did not look up. Hart went forward to watch, judging by the position of the wound that Pane's life was not in danger. After a few

131

moments, Wesley drew the bullet out of the wound. He looked up at Hart and nodded.

'He'll be OK in a week or so. What happened in the store?'

Hart explained while the doctor cleaned the wound and then bandaged it.

'So Ossie knows the dead coach-robber, huh?' Wesley shook his head. 'You just can't tell about people these days. I knew Ossie was cut up about young Billy's murder, and blamed K Bar. I guess he finally decided to do something about it, huh?'

'I'll know more about that after I've talked to him.' Hart replied.

'He'll come round shortly. I gave him just a whiff of anaesthetic because he was unconscious when I started on him.'

'I'll wait here with him, if that's OK by you,' Hart said.

'Sure. I'm going for coffee now. Can I get you one?'

'No thanks.' Hart sat down as Wesley departed, and tried to relax. Seifert arrived minutes later and bent over the unconscious storekeeper. He shook Payne's uninjured shoulder.

'Ossie, wake up!' he called. 'We need to talk. Come on. We ain't got all day.'

Payne stirred and his eyelids flickered. He groaned and opened his eyes, but for some moments could only gaze around without real awareness. Hart watched him intently and, when intelligence suddenly appeared in Payne's eyes, he moved in closer and bent over the man.

'You've got some explaining to do, Payne,' he said softly. 'Why did you reach for that shotgun when you saw me?'

'I knew by your expression that you had come for me,' Payne said slowly. 'I heard about the coach robber, and when I learned his description I knew it was Joe Bowman, my wife's brother. He came to stay with me when he got out of prison a week ago, and wanted to start hitting K Bar for killing my son Billy.'

'You didn't have any proof that the Kanes were responsible for Billy's death, Ossie,' Seifert protested. 'If there had been proof, the law would have dealt with them.'

'Who killed Luke Warner, Sarn and Thomas?' Hart asked.

'Joe did. He asked me for two hundred dollars, and reckoned to earn the dough by taking care of my problems. I didn't want anyone murdered, but when Joe killed Warner there was no other direction to go. Joe said that if he was caught he'd say I wanted him to do it. What happened yesterday? How did you catch up with Joe?'

'He ambushed Charlie Shaw the day before,' Hart said, 'and I followed his tracks until I caught up with him in the act of robbing the coach. Why did he ride into Rafter D and shoot up the place?'

'He knew Al Denton years ago. They rode with the same gang along the Mexican border, and Denton did him a good turn once. Joe was crooked through to his backbone, but he was the kind of man who didn't forget a favour. He told me a couple of days ago that Denton asked him to shoot up Rafter D.'

'Hey, stop right there, Ossie,' Seifert cut in. 'What was that about Denton asking Joe to shoot up Rafter D? Why in hell would he want a thing like that done?'

'That's what I asked, but Joe didn't say why. Denton asked him to do it and Joe just went ahead. He did say that Denton wanted a couple of his men shot up to make it look like someone really had it in for him.'

Hart exchanged glances with Seifert, who shrugged and grimaced.

'How did you link Joe with me?' Payne asked.

'You wrote him a banker's draft for two hundred dollars,' Hart said. 'The undertaker found it in his pocket. There is one thing that puzzles me. I trailed Joe to HR, and found a spot where someone on the ranch came out and spent some time with him. It was during the night before last. Joe was a stranger around here. Have you any idea who he knew at HR?'

'Flash Johnson. Joe said he was in jail with Flash about ten years ago. He saw Flash in town last week and they got together. Flash wanted a couple of jobs done. I tried to warn Joe off but he was all for making easy money.'

Hart moved away, satisfied that a number of the questions bothering him had been answered, but there were still more to be considered.

'I'm gonna jail you until I get the rights to this business,' Seifert said. 'You'll have to make a full statement, Ossie.'

Payne closed his eyes. Hart walked to the door and Seifert accompanied him.

'What happens now?' the deputy asked.

'I want to work on Grat Kane and Henry Reed, because if we can get rid of the bad blood between their outfits then the trouble should fizzle out. But we need to know why Al Denton wanted his place shot up, and what sort of jobs Flash Johnson got Joe to handle. If Joe knew Johnson and Denton then it is on the cards they knew each other. Someone is playing a deep game around here, and I'll check out these leads. How is Reed, by the way? Was he badly hurt in the shooting out at his place?'

'Doc patched him up, and said he should be OK in a couple of weeks.' Seifert heaved a sigh. 'This business is getting more complicated each day, and the thing I don't understand is why Denton would want his place shot up. It doesn't make sense.'

'It sounded to me like Denton wanted to put the blame for the shooting on someone else – HR or K Bar, probably,' Hart mused. 'What did Denton have to say when he came into town yesterday?'

'He said he had no idea who would have done such a thing to his spread. He had a couple of men killed, too!'

'I'll ride out to Rafter D now and ask Denton some questions,' Hart decided.

'Maybe I should go,' Seifert suggested, 'with a posse.'

'I also want to drop in at HR and have a talk with Flash Johnson.'

'Don't forget Wiley is on the loose now,' Seifert reminded.

'And Gimp Alder,' Hart added grimly.

He left the doctor's house and went along to the stable, his head whirling with conjecture. He saddled up, led the horse out to the water-trough and allowed it to drink. When hoofs pounded nearby he looked around to see three riders emerging from the stable. They had obviously entered through the back door. The foremost to appear was Grat Kane.

The big K Bar rancher rode up to where Hart was standing and reined in with the nose of his horse in Hart's face. Trig Dexter was on Kane's right, and another gunman flanked the rancher on the left. Hart grasped Kane's rein and pushed the big stallion's head away. The horse cavorted, then bucked a little, and for a moment Kane looked as if he was about to be thrown.

'Where's Wiley?' Hart demanded.

'Is that a joke?' Grat Kane looked surprised. 'He's in jail, where else?'

'What's going on?' Dexter asked. 'Has something happened to Wiley?'

'You kept me talking here at the stable last evening while some of your crew busted Wiley out of jail,' Hart said patiently. 'And they turned Gimp Alder loose. I can always pick up Wiley when I want him, but Alder is another matter. You went too far and broke the law, Kane, so I'm arresting you.'

'Arresting me?' Grat Kane bristled angrily, his eyes slitting. 'Trig, if this feller looks like he's gonna try such a fool thing then you got my permission to shoot him.' He spoke out of the side of his mouth, his dark gaze fastened hungrily on Hart's big figure.

'He's a Ranger, Grat,' Dexter said smoothly, 'and I

learned early in life not to tangle with his breed. If he wants to throw you in jail then he can, as far as I'm concerned.'

'You lily-livered skunk! I been paying you top wages for those two guns you're carrying, and the first time I ask you to back me you fold like a spineless jackass! OK, I don't need you to back my play. Get the hell out of my sight. You're finished around here.'

'It'll be my pleasure.' Dexter grinned tensely as he looked at the immobile Hart. 'Is it all right by you if I turn around and ride out?'

'Drop your guns on the ground and you're free to split the breeze,' Hart said. 'You can pick up your hardware later from the law office. Just be careful how you touch your butts. I'd say finger and thumb will be fine.'

Dexter nodded and disarmed himself, one gun at a time, then turned and rode back into the stable. Hart was watching the second gunman.

'What about you, mister?' he demanded. 'You got the same choice. Get rid of your gun and you're free to leave.'

'Nobody takes my gun.' The man's jaw champed steadily on a quid of tobacco.

'Then haul your hogleg and get to shooting.' Hart spoke softly but his voice seared through the silence with the scorch of a branding-iron. His tall, slab-muscled body was standing easily, hipshot, almost casual, but his unblinking gaze held the impersonal glitter of a snake watching its prey with the sure knowledge that it would succeed with its strike.

The gunman's right hand was poised above the butt of his holstered pistol. His eyes had the glassy stare of deadly intention. His jaw stopped chewing and sagged open, allowing tobacco juice to trickle down through the stubble on his chin. The fingers of his gun hand half-clenched convulsively and then relaxed. The next instant his slack jaw closed with a snap of teeth and his hand moved fast as he clawed for the butt of his pistol.

There was the rasp of metal against leather, the triple clicks of the gun being cocked as it swept up into the aim, and then the gunman paused, shockingly aware that he was not fast enough.

Hart's pistol was in his hand and levelled. It blasted even as the gunman realized his mistake, and he took that knowledge into hell with him when the .45 slug of lead tore through his heart. He jerked backwards, twisting lifelessly, and then pitched to the ground. Dust arose at the impact, and then began to settle as harsh echoes racketed across the silent town.

Grat Kane sat like a graven image, his big hands clenched tight upon his reins, holding his horse motionless with sheer brute strength. Disbelief was showing on his face. No one could be that fast, he was thinking, and yet he had witnessed Hart's draw.

'Are you bracing yourself to do your own fighting now?' Hart asked.

Kane shook his head, and when he spoke it sounded as if the spirit had gone out of him.

'I got no quarrel with the law,' he said jerkily. 'I've always lived within its framework. I guess my temper has brought me to this. Folk have given me a bad name and I've begun to act the part. Any man will go out on a limb for his own flesh and blood, but Wiley don't seem to be cut from the same cloth as me. He's got a wild streak that I ain't been able to tame, and I can see where he's heading if he don't pull in his horns. You'll kill him, Ranger.'

'I will, in the course of my duty, if I have to,' Hart agreed. 'Did you arrange Wiley's escape from jail?'

Grat Kane shook his head. 'It was a coincidence. I came into town to get you to release Wiley, not to bust him out. You'll have to look elsewhere for that culprit.'

'And I think I know where to look.' Hart nodded. 'Get your dead gunnie off the street, Kane, and then ride back to your place. I'll talk to you again when this business has been settled. Stay out of this local trouble. It would be a mistake to get involved.'

'I've got to find Wiley,' Kane protested. 'I'm the only one can handle him.'

Hart turned to his horse and saw Lew Seifert standing nearby, covering his back with a drawn pistol. The deputy shook his head as he holstered the gun and came forward.

'You're letting Grat off the hook?' he demanded.

'I don't think he's responsible for anything that's happened around here,' Hart said. 'In any case, I'll know where to find him should we want him. He ain't the kind to run. I reckon he'll be around for the final tally.'

'What happened to Trig Dexter? He ducked out of fighting you.'

'Take his guns to the office. I'm riding out. I'll

head for HR first and then swing off to Rafter D. I've learned enough to start things moving so I'd better get to it.'

'Sure thing.' Seifert stood in the street, shaking his head as he watched Hart's progress out of town.

Hart pushed his horse into a run when he was clear of Mesquite and rode steadily towards HR. He watched his surroundings alertly, aware that there were some desperate men in the county who were pushing their own particular interests with no consideration for their victims. He sensed that all the answers to the trouble hereabouts could be found at Rafter D, but he wanted to take care of some minor details before forcing a showdown with Al Denton.

He left the trail into the valley where HR was situated and rode along the rim to the east until he discovered a narrow game-trail which could be negotiated. He descended the trail to the valley floor and found himself behind the ranch house. He rode towards it steadily, checking his surroundings as he closed in.

He rode along the side of the house and reined in when he was able to scan the yard. Smoke was coming from the cook-shack, and he wondered if it was caused by the fire heating the oven or the food itself being burned. At that moment. Flash Johnson emerged from the house and stood on the porch looking around the yard. Hart kneed his horse forward a couple of steps. The HR ramrod caught the movement and whirled quickly, his hand dropping to the butt of his holstered pistol.

Johnson gazed at Hart as if he had seen a ghost.

His fleshy face was pinched and there was a glazed look of shock in his eyes.

'What in hell are you doing there?' Johnson called. 'How long have you been there?'

'Just rode in,' Hart replied. 'How is Henry Reed? I heard his wound is not too serious.'

'Bad enough for a man his age. Anything you want in particular?'

'I came to talk to you.' Hart rode around to the front of the house and stepped down to wrap his reins around the hitching-rail there. He turned and confronted Johnson, noting unmistakable signs of guilt in the man's expression. His mind ran over the information he had gained from Ossie Payne and knew how to apply it.

Johnson glanced around as Hart mounted the porch steps, his hand remaining close to the butt of his gun.

'How can I help you?' he demanded. 'This ain't a convenient time, what with the boss laid low.'

'Would you prefer to ride into town with me and be questioned in the jail?'

'The jail? What's been said about me?'

'I want you to tell me,' Hart said.

'If it's about my time in prison then I'll tell you. I haven't tried to conceal my past. Henry Reed knows all about it. He gave me a chance when I first came into this county, and I've repaid him by staying on the level and looking after his interests.'

'But all that changed when Joe Bowman showed up in Mesquite a week ago, huh?'

'Bowman?' Johnson shook is head. 'I've never

heard that name before.'

'That's strange, seeing that you and Bowman spent time in prison together about ten years ago.'

'Who told you that?'

'Ossie Payne. He's Bowman's brother-in-law. I guess you knew that, huh?'

Johnson moistened his lips. He had the expression of a hunted animal in his narrowed eyes, and drew a deep breath, shaking his head as he considered.

'You can't pay heed to anything Ossie Payne says,' he replied at length. 'He's loco. His son's death turned his mind. You're wasting my time, Ranger, and your own. If you're looking for the men causing the trouble in this county then you'll have to search elsewhere.'

'I know where to look for them,' Hart said grimly, 'and I'll be paying them a visit when I've finished my business here. What did you and Bowman talk about when you met under the big cottonwood on the other side of the valley a couple of nights ago? Were you trying to pull him into the local trouble or was he sounding you out about what he was doing?'

Johnson shook his head. 'Bowman is a lying skunk. I turned over a new leaf when I got out of prison, but Bowman stayed with it. He's a cold-blooded killer, and I told him I wanted no part of his crooked business.'

'He's dead now,' Hart said softly.

Johnson's shock increased. 'Dead? What happened to him?'

'I caught up with him robbing a coach. He must have had local information on that deal, and I

142

suspect you of filling him in.'

'Not me. I've been going straight for ten years. You can check that out quite easily.'

'So what about your business with Al Denton?'

'Denton! What's he got to do with anything?'

'I haven't talked to him yet but I'll get around to him shortly.'

'Did Bowman tell you I've been planning things with Denton?'

'You and Denton were in the same outlaw gang along the Mexican border years ago. I reckon you've renewed your acquaintance, and the trouble going on around here is the result. Whose idea was it to cause trouble for K Bar and HR and make it look like one or the other was responsible?'

'You're loco if you believe that.'

'I told you there are two ways of handling this,' Hart said patiently. 'Tell me about it here and now or we'll ride into town and talk in the jail.'

'You can't pin anything on me. I've kept my nose clean for ten years.'

'I'm not out to pin anything on anyone. I want the truth so I can nail the guilty men and put them where they belong.'

'Bowman was out here to see me the other night. I saw him in town earlier and he talked about cleaning up around here. I told him I'd go along with him but had no intention of doing so. I needed time to think how I could stay out of his game. He mentioned Denton's plans about hitting K Bar and HR to get them fighting each other, figuring to clean up while the two spreads were shooting one another.'

143

'You threw in with Denton long before Bowman turned up.' Hart tried a judicious shot in the dark, and saw Johnson's expression change.

'Denton asked me a long time ago to throw in with him, but I had turned over a new leaf and wouldn't change my mind. If Denton has told you otherwise then he's lying.' Johnson shook his head. 'I ain't put a foot wrong since I've been here.'

'Who shot Henry Reed yesterday?'

'I don't know. I thought Bowman did it.'

'It wasn't him. He was miles from here when the shooting happened.'

'Then you'll need to ask Denton about that. Him and Wiley Kane have been teamed up for months. Denton thought he was on to a good thing when Wiley threw in with him, but Wiley is a wild man and he's set on his own trail.'

'Which is?' Hart prompted.

'Ginny Reed. He's crazy about her. I've managed to keep him at a distance, but since Denton busted him out of jail last night he's gone right over the edge. It'll take a bullet now to stop to him. He rode in here last night demanding to see Ginny. I told him she was staying in Mesquite with a friend, but Wiley wouldn't leave until he'd searched the place, and then he rode off in a helluva mood.'

'Where is Ginny now?'

'Like I said; she rode into town to stay with her friend, Helen. I ain't seen her since. She often goes into town for a few days at a time. I didn't tell Wiley where she is in town, and Buck Dolan is with her. She never rides alone these days.'

144

Hart shook his head. 'I'm gonna accept what you've said, Johnson, because I got no proof against you,' he mused, 'so I'll leave you here for now, but I'll come for you if I learn that you've lied to me about anything.'

'I've told you the truth,' Johnson said harshly.

Hart went to his horse and swung into the saddle. He rode back across the yard and headed for the trail out of the valley. There was only one thing left for him to do now, and that was to confront Al Denton and get at the truth.

He was just clearing the valley when the sound of approaching hoofs alerted him. Hart rode into cover as a rider appeared, pounding along the trail from Mesquite. He spurred out into the open again when he recognized Buck Dolan, Ginny Reed's escort. The man was in a tearing hurry, which meant only one thing; Ginny Reed had to be in trouble.

TEN

Dolan pulled his horse to a dust-raising halt when he saw Hart. There was blood on his shirt front, his face was pale, and he was swaying in his saddle. His chin dropped to his chest as Hart reached him.

'Wiley's got Ginny,' Dolan said. 'He showed up in town, got the drop on me, and plugged me in cold blood after I dropped my gun. He had a horse for Ginny, and was riding out of town with her when Lew Seifert tried to stop him. Wiley shot him. The deputy is pretty bad. He said you were out here at HR and told me to warn you.'

'Have you any idea where Wiley went?' Hart demanded.

'He was with one of Al Denton's crew – Bill Frayne, Denton's top gun.' Dolan's voice trailed off and he slumped in the saddle. 'They rode out in the direction of Rafter D. As I left town to find you, Grat Kane and his crew were riding in.'

'Can you make it to HR?'

Dolan stirred himself. Blood was leaking from a wound in his left side just above the hip.

'I'll ride with you,' he said harshly. 'Ginny is my responsibility.'

'Not today. Get yourself patched up.' Hart heard the thud and echo of hoofs at his back and glanced over his shoulder to see Flash Johnson riding out of the valley. The foreman angled to his right and disappeared into a fold in the ground. 'I've got to be riding,' he added. 'Take care of yourself.'

Dolan sighed and slumped in his saddle. He shook his reins and went on along the trail towards the ranch. Hart swung his horse and moved after Johnson. There was a picture of Ginny Reed in his mind and a growing conviction that Wiley Kane could not turn from the trail he had taken. The big man was accustomed to getting his own way in everything, and would have to be shown the error of his ways.

The news that Wiley was in cahoots with Al Denton gave Hart a fresh angle on the trouble. He had suspected Grat Kane of running with an unknown gang, but now it seemed that Wiley was the guilty man. If Grat had been telling the truth about not breaking his son out of jail then Denton must have been responsible.

Flash Johnson was riding fast, oblivious to his surroundings, and Hart slipped in behind him and followed at a discreet distance. The ramrod rode fast for a couple of hours, and Hart recognized landmarks. He had trailed Joe Bowman through here in the opposite direction, and was now getting close to the line shack between Rafter D and HR, where he had wounded Sam Wishart a couple of days ago.

147

When the dilapidated shack appeared ahead, Hart reined into cover and watched Johnson dismount in front of it. A man stepped into the doorway, and there was no mistaking him. It was Wiley Kane, holding a rifle cradled in his arms and looking as if he was prepared to fight the whole world.

'What are you doing here, Johnson?' Wiley boomed in a gravelled tone. 'Is Reed dead yet?'

'He ain't nearly dead.' Johnson shook his head, and his next words gave the listening Hart all he needed to know. 'It was a bad job. He should have been killed. Did you get the girl?'

'Sure I got her.' Wiley grinned. 'I took her off the street with hardly a witness. I only had to shoot Dolan, and then put Seifert down when he tried to stick his nose in. You better go back to HR and put another slug in Reed.'

'I can't do that. The Ranger dropped by earlier. He knew a lot about the business. He killed Bowman, and shot Ossie Payne, who's done a lot of talking.'

'Where's the Ranger now?' Wiley gripped his rifle and made a threatening gesture with it. 'Just let him show his face round here. I'll do what I should have done when I first laid eyes on him. I guessed he'd make trouble.'

'I think he was riding to Rafter D when he left me. Denton is gonna be in a lot of trouble if the law starts horning in.'

'Then you better ride over there and warn him. We've got to kill a few men to keep this business quiet, and the sooner Denton gets on with that the better.'

Johnson shrugged and swung into his saddle. He sat for a moment looking down at Wiley.

'You know you can't let Ginny live when this is over, don't you?' he demanded.

'You leave the girl be. She won't give us any trouble. Now get the hell out of here. What are you sitting there for when there's killing to be done?'

Johnson shook his head and turned away. Hart watched the ramrod until he had disappeared over a ridge. Wiley lifted his rifle and aimed at Johnson's back, grinning as he did so. For a moment, Hart thought the big man was about to shoot Johnson, but Wiley lowered the weapon, turned, and went back into the shack.

Hart led his horse back into deeper cover and tethered it to a bush. He checked his pistol before moving away cautiously, circling to the rear of the shack.

There were two horses in the corral behind the building, and Hart recognized one of them as the animal that Ginny rode. Hart watched the animals for some moments, waiting until he was satisfied that Wiley was alone, and then sneaked in towards the rear of the shack.

Silence was heavy around him, and Hart dared not betray his presence. He got down and crawled over the last few yards, and finally paused with his head almost touching the weather-beaten boards of the back wall. There were holes aplenty in the rotting woodwork, and he got up on one knee and peered through a knot-hole. The interior of the shack was gloomy, and it was some moments before he could see the gross figure of Wiley Kane seated at a table. The big man was cleaning his rifle.

Hart looked around for Ginny, eventually spotting her lying on a bunk on the far side of the shack. Hart compressed his lips at the sight of her. There was no one else in the shack, and he eased back out of earshot and pushed himself to his feet.

Johnson had intimated that Ginny had to be killed, and Wiley would have no compunction in disposing of the girl, despite his apparent interest in her. Hart drew his pistol and moved around the shack. It was time to put an end to Wiley Kane's crooked business.

He circled the shack at a distance, wary of letting his shadow fall upon the walls for fear of alerting Wiley. When at last he faced the open doorway, he was ten feet clear of the little building. He started to move in, gun levelled at his hip. He wanted to get the drop on Wiley, for any stray shooting might hit Ginny.

He was half-way to the door when a gun fired from his left rear and he felt the smash of a bullet in his left arm just above the elbow. The impact spun him around, and as the silence was shattered by the blast of the shot he saw Flash Johnson standing twenty feet away, grinning as he aligned his pistol for a second shot.

Hart dropped to the ground, firing as he did so, aiming instinctively. He jarred his arm making contact with the ground, but his gaze was fastened on Johnson, who suddenly dropped his pistol and folded jerkily to thrust his face into the dust. Hart twisted around to face the door of the shack, his worry for Ginny taking precedence in his mind. Gun echoes were already fading away into the vast distance. He clenched his teeth against darting pain and pushed himself to his feet.

Wiley Kane stepped into the doorway with levelled rifle. He was grinning as if the whole business were a joke. Hart was just out of arm's length.

'I been expecting you to show up,' Wiley growled. 'I always knew I'd have to kill you, and I owe you for the way you and Seifert beat me up the other night.'

'Drop the rifle and throw up your hands,' Hart said. 'I told your pa I wouldn't kill you unless it was in the line of duty.'

'I can't do that. I got too much to lose.'

Hart could tell that Wiley had no intention of surrendering. He kicked out suddenly with his right foot, and the toe of his boot smacked under Wiley's left hand where it was grasping the stock of the Winchester. Wiley let out a yell as the rifle was forced to his left. His trigger finger tightened convulsively, firing a shot. Hart stepped in close as Wiley tried to swing the long gun back to cover him, and crashed the barrel of his pistol into the big man's face.

Wiley stepped back into the shack, trying desperately to bring his rifle to bear. Hart slammed his pistol across Wiley's left hand and it fell away from the rifle. Following up, Hart kicked the big man in the belly, and Wiley yelled and went down, shaking the shack to its rotting foundations.

Wiley, flat on his back, was reaching for his holstered pistol. Hart paused and levelled his Colt.

'Don't do it,' Hart warned. 'Don't make me kill you, Wiley.'

The big man ignored the warning. His clutching fingers closed on the butt of his gun and dragged it out of the holster. Hart fired, his shot blasting out the silence, making his ears ring in the confines of the shack. Wiley's gun hand was shattered by the .45 slug and fell away; the pistol flipping out of his reach. Wiley screeched in pain and flopped back like a gut-shot moose.

Wiley lifted his feet in the air and tried to kick Hart, who moved out of range and glanced towards the bunk where Ginny Reed was lying. He saw a rope tied around the girl's ankles. She was pale-faced in shock, her eyes wide, but she forced a wan smile as Hart turned his attention to her.

'You'll have to kill Wiley to stop him,' she advised.

Hart glanced at the big man, who was gripping his shattered right hand in the big paw of his left hand. Blood was seeping through his thick fingers.

'He's too busy at the moment to worry about me.' Hart crossed to the bunk and untied the girl. 'Can you stand? You've got to split the breeze out of here.'

He helped her upright. She swayed, but kept her balance as Hart led her to the door.

'Get on your horse and head back to HR,' he directed. 'I killed Flash Johnson a few minutes ago.' He saw fresh shock appear on her face, and nodded. 'Johnson was mixed up in this, along with Al Denton.'

'I can't run out on you,' she said firmly. 'Your arm is bleeding badly.'

'I'll take care of it the minute you're in the clear,' he responded. 'I can't escort you back to HR. I've got to finish my job, and the end of it will be at Rafter D.'

'I know. I heard Wiley talking to Gimp Alder, who was waiting for Wiley out of town after he took me. Denton's outfit busted Wiley and Alder out of jail, and Wiley took a liking to Alder. They were making big plans for the future.'

'Where did Alder go?'

'He left us a couple of miles from here, saying something about looking you up.'

'That sounds like Gimp.' Hart nodded. 'He would try to settle personal issues when he should be running as far as a horse can take him, because I'll get on his trail again when I've settled the trouble around here.' He turned his attention to Wiley. 'Why didn't you leave that outlaw behind bars? He's not the kind of man you can do a deal with, and wouldn't lift a hand to help you.'

'That's where you're wrong, Ranger.' Wiley grinned and pointed with his chin towards the open doorway. 'I can see Alder out there. He's waiting for you to show yourself.'

Hart moved swiftly to the glassless window beside the door and peered out. His eyes narrowed at the sight of Gimp Alder crouching over Johnson's body, searching the dead ramrod's pockets. The outlaw was holding a pistol, and straightened as Hart drew his Colt.

'I got you covered, Alder. Throw down that gun, lift your hands and come on over here.'

Alder fired instantly, and the bullet plucked at the

wide brim of Hart's Stetson. As the report of the shot rang out, Hart returned fire, triggering two shots, and Alder spun and fell to the ground. He raised himself slightly, trying to bring his pistol to bear, and Hart fired again. The bullet dusted the outlaw's jacket in the centre of the chest, and Alder slumped to the sun-baked ground.

'Thanks for the warning, Wiley,' Hart said.

'Thank you,' Wiley replied. 'I wanted that dumb-cluck dead. He figured to start running things around here. You've just done me a big favour.'

Hart heard the sound of approaching hoofs and grasped Ginny's arm.

'Riders coming,' he said. 'You should have got out of here while you had the chance.'

'Who are they?' She had turned her attention to Hart's arm. 'If you don't have this attended to, you'll likely bleed to death.'

'Forget it.' Hart was gazing at four riders who came into view.

Ginny looked out of the window.

'They're HR crew,' she said excitedly. 'Buck Dolan is leading them.' She craned forward and stuck her head through the glassless aperture. 'Hey, Buck, over here,' she called.

The four riders came across to the shack. Hart recognized Dolan. The puncher was pale-faced and there were bloodstains on his shirt. He slid out of his saddle and, as he staggered to the doorway, a rifle blasted from somewhere nearby. Dolan fell against a doorpost, pitched to the ground, and lay motionless on the threshold of the shack.

'Get down!' Hart yelled at the girl, and ran to drag Dolan into the scant cover of the little building. He saw fresh blood dribbling from the puncher's right shoulder. 'See if you can help Dolan,' he said to Ginny, 'and keep your head down while you're doing it.'

Pandemonium erupted outside as the other three HR riders sprang from their saddles and came bustling into the shack.

'They are Rafter D punchers shooting at us,' one of them announced.

Hart picked up the Winchester Wiley had dropped earlier. He glanced outside, and saw figures moving around some twenty yards in front of the shack. In the background, a man was peeping around a tree, and Hart recognized Al Denton.

'Hey, you in the shack,' Denton called. 'Come on out with your hands up or we'll come in and get you.'

'I'm Mike Hart, Texas Ranger,' Hart replied. 'Throw down your guns and surrender to the law.'

'I know who you are. Come on out or we'll come in,' Denton repeated.

'Talk is cheap,' one of the HR crew shouted. 'Come and get us.'

Shooting started and heavy echoes hammered away. Hart was satisfied that Denton was aware the law was present.

Ginny uttered a cry of alarm and Hart glanced around. The girl was crouching low over Dolan, and Wiley had seized hold of her ankle. Hart hurried across and kicked Wiley's injured right hand. The big man cursed and turned away. Hart returned his attention to the attack that Denton was organizing. He saw more of the Rafter D crew in the background, circling on either side to surround the shack. Gunfire blasted and slugs began splintering through the walls of the little building.

Hart watched for Denton, but the Rafter D rancher was no longer in view. More than a dozen men were shooting into the shack and bullets were passing easily through the walls. Hart was concerned for the girl, but she had enough sense to stay low. None of them could return fire, for to get up to shoot would be inviting death from any of the dozens of shots hammering into the place.

Hart glanced around the shack and spotted a shuttered window in the rear wall. He crawled to it and lifted a wooden bar to release the shutter. Ginny was watching him and he made signs indicating that he would leave the shack and take the fight to Rafter D. She shook her head in horror, but Hart knew he had little time in which to consider. He lunged to his feet and hurled himself out through the aperture.

His left arm struck the side of the aperture as he passed through and he fell heavily to the ground outside. He rolled quickly and rose to a sitting position, lifting the Winchester clutched in his right hand. He could see men circling the shack on either side and lifted the rifle to open fire, hoping Wiley had reloaded the weapon fully after cleaning it.

Shooting to the left, Hart nailed three men in quick succession, and turned his attention to the right as fire began coming at him from that side. He triggered the rifle as fast as he could work the mechanism, shifting his aim, slamming lead into the flitting figures closing in. Counting his shots, he fired ten before the rifle was empty. Then he discarded it and drew his pistol.

He pushed himself to his feet and looked around. There were no more targets to his right and he eased towards the left-hand corner of the shack. A puncher came around the corner just as Hart reached it. Hart fired, and the man went down with blood spouting from a wound that appeared in his throat. Hart peered around the corner and triggered his pistol at two men along the side, cutting them down as he went on.

A sudden increase in the rate of fire in front of the shack worried Hart and he hurried forward to take a look around the front corner. He was surprised when the shooting stopped abruptly just as he reached the corner. He flattened against the wall and risked a look out front.

Denton's surviving crew were pulling back, and Hart was surprised to see the huge figure of Grat Kane sitting his big horse in a fringe of trees thirty yards away. His outfit were covering the Rafter D men, having sneaked in from their rear. Hart took the opportunity to reload his smoking pistol.

'What's going on, Kane?' he called.

Grat Kane wheeled his mount and came across the rough ground. He was holding a shotgun across his saddle horn and the twin barrels were covering Hart.

'I heard in town what my boy did earlier,' Grat called. 'Is he here, Ranger?'

'He's here,' Hart replied.

'Is the girl all right?'

'She's fine.'

'Wiley didn't harm her?'

'No.'

'And did you kill Wiley?'

'He's still alive. I had to bust his gun hand, but he'll patch up. Come and take a look at him.'

Grat Kane swung down from his saddle and Hart went out to join him. The K Bar rancher looked around, shaking his head.

'I heard in town what had happened and reckoned to come in on your side,' he growled. 'I've had my doubts about Denton for a long time, but couldn't get any proof of his doings. It looks like you didn't need any help. You were doing all right on your own.'

Ginny appeared in the doorway of the shack. She was clutching a pistol in her right hand and a wisp of smoke was curling up from the barrel. Hart holstered his gun. He was feeling exhausted, and there was great pain in his left arm. His mind flitted over the whole business and he could not think of a single question that remained unanswered, aware that no more questions meant the case was closed.

'You know Wiley will have to stay in jail until his trial, huh?' he remarked.

Grat Kane laughed hollowly.

'Heck, I wouldn't dare raise that subject now,' he declared. 'Anyway, I've always tried to get along with the law.'

Kane went into the shack and Hart heard him shouting at his son. Ginny came to his side and took hold of his left arm, shaking her head.

'Perhaps we can do something about this now,' she said.

'Sure.' Hart relaxed. His work here was finished, and he was already composing his report for head-quarters as the girl attended to his wound.